THE HAPPINESS PATROL

DOCTOR WHO
THE HAPPINESS PATROL

based on the BBC television series by Graeme Curry
by arrangement with BBC Books, a division of BBC
Enterprises Ltd

GRAEME CURRY

Number 146 in the
Target Doctor Who Library

A TARGET BOOK
published by
the Paperback Division of
W H Allen & Co Plc

A Target Book
Published in 1990
By the Paperback Division of
W H Allen & Co Plc
Sekforde House, 175/9 St John Street, London EC1V 4LL

The BBC producer was John Nathan-Turner
The director was Chris Clough
The role of the Doctor was played by Sylvester McCoy

Printed and bound in Great Britain by
Cox & Wyman Ltd, Reading

ISBN 0 426 20339 9

1

The woman wanted to die. When the Happiness Patrol had taken away her husband she had at first refused to give in, for the sake of her son. But now that her son had disappeared, along with thousands of other innocent victims, she had nothing left to live for. She wrapped her dark cape around her and trudged down the street. She didn't know where she was going and she didn't care.

'Over here,' said a voice that seemed to come from nowhere.

Peering through the gloom she could just make out a bench beneath a streetlight, and on the bench a shadowy figure.

'You need to rest.'

The voice sounded friendly and inviting. The woman moved to the bench and sat down.

'That's better.' The kindness was too much to endure. The tears came suddenly, flowing down her cheeks in great cascades.

'Here.' The figure on the bench lowered the newspaper he was reading and offered her his handkerchief. Through the blur of her tears, the woman could make out a man in a trilby. He was dressed, like her, in dark, drab clothes. She saw that the newspaper was a copy of *The Grief*, the killjoy undercover publication. So he was one of the killjoys. She knew she was safe with him.

'Do you want to talk about it?' His voice was gentle.

'I don't talk to strangers.'

He ignored the bitterness in her voice. 'Perhaps I can help.'

'I didn't ask for any help.'

'But we both know you can't sit here like this,' said the man in the trilby. 'It's dangerous.'

'It's too late,' she replied. 'I don't care any more. Let them find me.'

There was silence for a few moments, as she dried her tears. Then the man spoke softly to her.

'You don't have to face your suffering alone, you know.'

'What do you mean?' she asked.

'There's a place,' he said, 'a secret place, where some of us go to indulge our depressions, to share our miseries with other killjoys like you and me.'

She knew she was a killjoy, but refused to admit it, even to herself. 'I am not a killjoy!'

'That's what they would call you,' said the man. 'Are you interested?'

She suddenly realized that here was a way of avenging the deaths in her family – she could fight for the killjoys. She had nothing to lose, but she remained cautious. 'Perhaps,' she said.

The man smiled. 'It changed my life.' He reached into his coat. 'Look, here's my card.' The woman hesitated. 'Go on. Take it.'

Taking the card, she read the name embossed in black ink. 'Silas P.'

'No,' said Silas P, 'look at the other side.'

She turned over the card and stared in disbelief at the words before her. 'But it says . . .'

'Happiness Patrol,' barked Silas P triumphantly, 'undercover!' Before the woman had time to react, Silas P blew into a small silver whistle. The harsh tone echoed in the empty street. Silas P removed the whistle from his mouth and smiled gently at the woman.

'Time to get really depressed!' he said.

As he spoke, a military jeep rounded the corner and screeched to a halt before them. The woman briefly saw the

6

uniforms of the Happiness Patrol before she was blinded by the powerful arc lights that were trained on her. Daisy K, the patrol lieutenant, stepped out of the jeep and aimed her fun gun at the terrified woman.

'Have a nice death!' she said.

The Happiness Patrol opened fire.

Ace stepped out of the TARDIS. They seemed to be in a town square that was dominated by an imposing building with steps leading up to its doors. Next to it she saw a small scruffy doorway with the words STAGE DOOR painted above it. Perhaps the building was a concert hall or theatre. She glanced around the rest of the square. At first sight it seemed a cheerful sort of place, painted in bright colours. But when she looked closer, she could see that the paint was faded; in some places it was peeling off the walls. Opposite the theatre there were two huge faces painted on the wall, one happy, one sad. The scene reminded her of something from her childhood.

The Doctor was thinking about dinosaurs, his mind still on a recent conversation with Ace. 'How about a triceratops?' he said, coming out of the TARDIS.

'A triceratops?' said Ace. She could never remember which dinosaurs were which.

'Horned dinosaur with a mouth like a beak. The Brigadier saw one in the London Underground,' said the Doctor by way of explanation.

Ace wanted to meet a dinosaur. 'Have you seen a tyrannosaurus rex?' she asked.

'I've met quite a few, actually,' he said.

'Wicked!' said Ace, her eyes shining. 'And pterodactyls?'

The Doctor was getting bored. 'Lots of pterodactyls, Ace.'

'Evil!'

'Maybe we should pay a little visit sometime,' said the Doctor.

'To the Earth?' said Ace. 'During the Cretaceous period?'

'It would be a good time for dinosaurs,' said the Doctor, looking round the square.

'I love dinosaurs,' said Ace wistfully, 'but I hate that.' There were several ornate loudspeakers in the square: one hung from a beautifully fashioned wrought-iron balcony; another was fastened to a pale blue wall high above them. They were broadcasting music across the square, but it was not real music – not music with any kind of feeling or passion. Ace remembered this kind of music from the London of the 1980s, where it pervaded department stores, shopping centres, hotels and waiting rooms.

'Lift music,' she snorted contemptuously. Suddenly she didn't like this planet very much. 'Where are we, Professor?'

'Terra Alpha,' said the Doctor. 'What do you mean, lift music?'

'Like they play in lifts,' said Ace impatiently. For a Time Lord, there were surprising gaps in the Doctor's knowledge. 'What's Terra Alpha, anyway?'

'A planet,' said the Doctor. 'An Earth colony settled some centuries in your future. Do you like it?'

'No.'

'Neither do I. Why not?'

'Too phoney,' said Ace. She now knew what it reminded her of. Years ago her parents had taken her to a pantomime in Ealing. She had loved it. After the show, she was allowed to walk on the stage and look at the scenery. She discovered that the emperor's palace was a crudely painted backcloth and that the magic lamp was an old tin can bent into shape. She felt cheated. That was what Terra Alpha reminded her of: the crumbling illusion. She felt cheated again.

The Doctor was speaking: 'Yes, I've been hearing disturbing rumours about Terra Alpha. I decided I'd look in some time.'

'So tonight's the night?' Ace was ready.

'Tonight's the night,' said the Doctor. 'Rumours of something evil, Ace. We have to find out what's behind it all.'

* * *

8

Silas P knelt before Helen A as she fastened a small badge to his tunic. They were in the headquarters of the Happiness Patrol, a small room in the heart of the palace – the nerve centre of Terra Alpha.

'Your third badge, Silas P,' said Helen A. 'Forty-five killjoys to your credit. Impressive work – I'm very happy.'

'I'm glad you're happy,' said Silas P. But Helen A, although his superior and, indeed, the governor of Terra Alpha, was not always right. 'But it's forty-seven, actually.'

'I do the counting, thank you, Silas,' snapped Helen A, irritated by his presumption.

'Sorry, ma'am.'

'Still, I like your initiative, your enterprise,' said Helen A. She was genuinely impressed with Silas's dedication. The Happiness Patrol needed more members with his single-mindedness. 'I'll see that you go far.'

Silas had never had such an intimate conversation with Helen A before, and was encouraged to confide in her. 'I'm aiming at the top,' he said.

This, however, was a mistake. Helen A had always admired ambition, but not when it threatened her supremacy. 'Not quite the very top, I hope, Silas,' she said mildly.

Silas P was dismissed and Helen A moved through her personal suite of rooms. She observed with distaste Joseph C, her consort, slumped in front of a television set.

'What are you watching?' she asked.

Joseph C came to with a start. He consulted a box on the arm of the chair. 'It's a video of something called "Routine disappearance number four hundred and ninety-nine thousand and eighty-seven".'

Helen A glanced at the monitor. She saw the screaming face of Silas P's latest victim in a huge close-up, moments before her death.

'Switch it off, dear,' she said. 'That's for my eyes only. And besides, we're missing my broadcast.'

She scooped up the remote control and changed the television channel. She smiled as an image of herself filled the screen. She was pleased with what she saw. Her image consultants had done her proud. She listened to her soft voice intoning her weekly address to her citizens.

'Finally, Joseph C and I would like to thank you all for your sterling work in helping to track down the killjoys and report them to the authorities,' said the image. 'I would also like to take this opportunity to squash the persistent rumours about mysterious "disappearances" and emphasize that rural and urban areas are now enjoying a life of harmony and peace. I'm sure you're glad to hear this. And I'm happy you're glad.'

Helen A was pleased with the effect of this speech, and was concentrating on the screen, but saw Joseph C out of the corner of her eye, trying to slip unnoticed out of the room. 'I think you should watch this, darling,' she said pleasantly. Joseph C moved quickly back to his chair. 'You'll find it instructive.' Helen A returned to the monitor. Her image was ending the speech. 'So remember – enjoy yourselves! Happiness will prevail!'

2

Ace's feet were beginning to hurt. They seemed to have walked for miles but they still couldn't escape from the lift music – the loudspeakers were everywhere.

'This music's winding me up, Professor,' she said.

The Doctor agreed. 'Makes you wonder how the natives can stand it.'

Ace suddenly realized that they hadn't seen a soul, human or alien, since they had arrived on Terra Alpha. 'I haven't seen any natives,' she said.

'There's one,' said the Doctor. A small dapper man in a bowler hat and dark suit was approaching. He was dressed soberly apart from a bright yellow tie, and was carrying a clipboard. He pointed at Ace.

'Name?' he asked.

'Ace,' she said, taken by surprise.

'No nicknames, aliases, pseudonyms, noms de plume,' said the man. 'Real name.'

This made Ace angry. 'That is my real name,' she protested. 'Tell him, Professor.'

'What's in a name?' mused the Doctor.

The man in the bowler hat turned sharply towards the Doctor. 'I could report you for that,' he said.

Ace was getting tired of this conversation, mainly because the air was suddenly filled with a delicious smell quite unlike anything Ace had smelt before. It made her realize how hungry she was.

'Can you smell something, Professor?' she asked.

'Now you mention it . . .' said the Doctor.

11

'It smells good, whatever it is,' Ace shouted back over her shoulder as she wandered off to investigate the smell, leaving the man in the bowler hat annoyed that his interview had been rudely ended. The Doctor tried to pacify him.

'I'm sorry about Ace, Mr . . . you didn't tell me your name.'

'You're right, I didn't,' said the man. 'But I don't have to – I'm on official business from Galactic Centre.'

The Doctor looked suspicious. 'How do I know you're telling the truth?' he asked.

The man produced a card and handed it to the Doctor. 'My identification.'

'Thank you . . . Trevor Sigma,' said the Doctor. Trevor Sigma looked surprised. 'Your name's on the card,' said the Doctor, by way of explanation. 'Actually, my nickname at college was Theta Sigma.'

'No nicknames.'

The Doctor returned the card to Trevor Sigma. 'If you're from the Galactic Centre you must be conducting a census of Terra Alpha.'

'Enquiries of that nature have to be referred to the appropriate department at the Galactic Centre. Messages may be left at weekends, except in emergencies in which case the sector manager is available . . .'

'Well, it's been lovely talking to you,' interrupted the Doctor, 'but Ace is probably in danger by now.' He doffed his hat. 'Bye now!'

The Doctor correctly guessed that Ace had left them in pursuit of the delicious smell. Finding that it came from a door marked 'Kandy Kitchen' he slipped inside and found himself in a large, steam-filled room with banks of ovens along one wall and a large stove in the centre, on which sat several boiling cauldrons. Thousands of pipes ran across the ceiling and the walls, on one of which slowly turned a network of large cogs. In the floor there were two metal manhole covers. Prominent on one of the kitchen shelves was a plastic skull, and on another the Doctor saw a hollow pumpkin.

Ace was at the far side of the room examining a heavy lever fastened to the stone floor. She called across to the Doctor: 'Professor, what do you think happens if I pull this?'

Just as the lever started to move, the Doctor was at her side, catching her hand and pushing the lever back to its original position. 'I don't know, Ace,' he said. 'And I don't intend to find out just yet.'

'Oh, Professor!'

'Anyway, I thought you came in here because you were hungry.'

Ace was again aware of the gnawing feeling in her stomach. 'Yeah, that's right.' She started to walk towards one of the ovens, but on instinct the Doctor held her back. He turned around to see one of the manhole covers slide into place: something had been watching them.

'What is it, Professor?' asked Ace, who had not seen anything.

'Nothing.'

In another part of the City, Earl Sigma played the blues on his harmonica. He was standing in the shadows, hat down over his eyes, his shoulders hunched. The haunting music echoed round the empty street. Suddenly he stopped and listened – he could hear the unmistakable sound of one of the Happiness Patrol's jeeps. He flicked his hat from his eyes and took up his harmonica again. This time the music was different – a trifling melody, going nowhere. Inconsequential and bland, it was just the sort of music the Happiness Patrol liked.

He was just in time. The jeep pulled over beside him and Daisy K jumped down. She regarded him suspiciously as she listened to the music, but eventually her foot began to tap and a smile crept across her face. After a few moments, she walked over to Earl Sigma and stuck a smile badge on his lapel – he had pleased her. She walked back to the jeep.

'To Forum Square,' she barked at the driver.

Forum Square was right at the centre of the city. If

Helen A wished to address her people she would speak to them from the steps in Forum Square. Once a year, on Liberation Day, she would inspect the Happiness troops and lead the singing of the patriotic song. But most important in Forum Square was the Forum building itself. The Terra Alphan people loved to be entertained and it was to the Forum that they would flock in their thousands to see the latest show.

The Happiness Patrol jeep stopped in Forum Square during the curfew, when everything was quiet. But something was different – a small blue dwelling had been erected in the corner. Daisy K circled warily round it.

'Do we have a bomb detector in the jeep?' she asked.

'Yes, ma'am,' said the driver.

'Then don't just sit there,' said Daisy K. 'Start detecting!'

The Doctor and Ace had still not come across any life-form, apart from the strange man in the yellow tie called Trevor Sigma. Ace was examining the bench on which Silas P's recent victim had met her fate.

'Well?' asked the Doctor.

'Bullet holes?'

'Definitely. This way.'

Ace followed the Doctor down a small passageway and they found themselves in a small yard, which was decorated with ribbons and bunting. Bunches of balloons hung in the corners, and a huge red waste-pipe, whch dominated the yard, was set into one of the walls.

'Looks like someone's having a party,' said Ace, idly bursting one of the balloons. 'Can we go to it, Professor?'

'We haven't been invited, Ace.'

'We can crash it.'

'We don't crash parties.' The Doctor had been poking his umbrella into the waste-pipe. Now he examined the strange substance on the umbrella tip. 'And we especially don't crash this one.'

14

Ace sulked while the Doctor tasted the substance. 'It's sweet,' he said.

'Sweet?' said Ace.

'Something very nasty is happening here,' said the Doctor, 'and we must put a stop to it – quckly.'

'How quickly?'

'Tonight.'

Ace perked up. 'Is this going to be dangerous?'

'Yes,' said the Doctor, tapping the waste-pipe with his umbrella. It gave a hollow ring.

'Right,' said Ace, looking forward to a bit of action. 'How do we start?'

'I think we'll get ourselves arrested,' said the Doctor.

Trevor Sigma had made his way to the Kandy Kitchen. He had first met Gilbert M on his last visit to Terra Alpha and had liked him immediately. Trevor did not enjoy the gaiety and flamboyance of Terra Alpha. He was much happier poring over statistics in the grey, faceless rooms of the Galactic Centre. So it was a relief to him to find in Gilbert M someone who seemed to share his enthusiasm for facts. Trevor knew that Gilbert was a scientist and that he worked in the Kandy Kitchen, and that was all that was required for his census so that was enough for Trevor.

He was sitting in the Kandy Kitchen telling Gilbert about new developments at the Galactic Centre.

'Restructuring?' asked Gilbert M.

'The whole bureau,' said Trevor. 'From top to bottom.'

'I envy you, Trevor,' said Gilbert.

Trevor Sigma warmed to his theme. 'Ten thousand new grades have been created and every decision now has to pass through five hundred new committees. You can imagine the extra paperwork!' Trevor's eyes gleamed – he loved paperwork.

'You must be thrilled,' said Gilbert M. He didn't much like paperwork, but he liked Trevor and was happy to please him.

15

'The bureau's moving into uncharted territory, Gilbert,' said Trevor. 'I'm just happy to be aboard.'

'Exciting,' said Gilbert. But time was pressing and Helen A had ordered a large batch of sweets. 'It's been nice talking to you, Trevor,' he said, 'but I'd better be getting back to work.'

'There is one other thing,' said Trevor. 'You remember last time I came to Terra Alpha I was unable to interview a certain person. I thought if I tried agan he might be more co-operative.'

Gilbert M knew that Trevor was talking about the Kandy Man. 'I don't know,' he sighed. 'A certain person is becoming increasingly difficult to handle.'

'Is he indeed?' said a deep, mellifluous voice. It was the Kandy Man. He was tall and powerfully built, dressed in a white lab coat and white trousers. He wore red-framed spectacles and a red bow-tie. Several red and white striped pens protruded from the pocket of his coat. His skin was pale and was covered with a soft white powder. As he moved towards them there was a soft, sucking sound as his feet touched the floor.

Trevor Sigma laughed nervously. 'Kandy Man!' he said, as jovially as he could.

The Kandy Man stifled a yawn. 'A certain person's patience is wearing thin.' His voice was gentle but firm. 'Now go!'

Trevor Sigma scuttled across the Kandy Kitchen and out into the street.

'It was just a few questions,' remonstrated Gilbert M.

The Kandy Man raised a powdery eyebrow. 'I don't give interviews,' he said.

3

'Professor!' shouted Ace. 'Look what they've done to the TARDIS!'

She could not believe her eyes – the TARDIS was pink. From the shadows of Forum Square they had a clear view of the Happiness Patrol carrying their pots of paint and putting the final touches to their work. Daisy K stood some distance from the others, overseeing the job.

'I think it looks rather good,' sad the Doctor. 'Come on.' He left their hiding place, closely followed by Ace, and walked over to Daisy K. She saw them immediately, raised her fun gun and turned towards Ace.

'You look unhappy about something,' she said.

'On the contrary,' said the Doctor quickly. 'We were just admiring your handiwork.' He nodded at the TARDIS. 'Miserable looking thing, wasn't it?'

'Our feeling exactly,' said Daisy K. She turned back to Ace. 'And what about you? Are you happy?'

Ace was about to speak when the Doctor interrupted her again. 'I would say so. Relatively speaking, she is. Given the deeply distressing nature of so many universal truths.'

Daisy K was getting angry. 'What do you mean?'

'She's happy,' said the Doctor. 'And I'm happy.'

Ace was tired of this exchange, nor did she like being threatened by a woman in a paramilitary uniform with a toy gun. 'Can't you afford a real gun?' said Ace.

Daisy K spun lightly on the balls of her feet and opened fire. Fifty yards away an ornate streetlamp exploded into a thousand pieces. Ace was impressed. 'Wicked!' she said, under her breath.

Daisy K faced them once more. 'I'm glad you're happy,' she said. 'I won't have to lock you up.' The Doctor looked disappointed. 'But why are you here?' continued Daisy K. 'You don't look like locals.' She regarded them closely. 'In fact, you look like killjoys.'

'We're visitors,' said the Doctor. 'Just here for the night.'

'Who are the killjoys?' asked Ace.

Daisy K was surprised. 'You really don't know? You must be from offworld.' The aggression went out of her voice. 'All right, in future stay in the specifed tourist zones.'

The Doctor was puzzled. 'Sorry?'

'You may go,' said Daisy K slowly and clearly. It was like talking to children.

'You're not going to arrest us?' asked Ace.

'I don't see why.'

'They're not going to arrest us, Doctor,' said Ace. The plan wasn't working.

'Badges,' said the Doctor.

'Badges?' said Ace.

The Doctor caught the attention of Daisy K, who had gone back to watching work in progress on the TARDIS.

'I believe all offworld personnel are issued with badges at customs,' he said.

'That's right.' Daisy K realized with embarrassment that she had overlooked this. 'Where are your badges?'

'I've got badges,' said Ace, proudly displaying the front of her leather jacket.

'She's got badges,' said the Doctor.

Ace pointed out a particular badge. 'This one's Charlton Athletic.'

Daisy K's patience was wearing thin. 'Not interested,' she said, through clenched teeth. 'And you – where's your badge?'

The Doctor examined his jacket. 'Oh dear. I don't seem to have one.'

Daisy K's patience snapped. She clicked her fingers and two members of the Happiness Patrol ran to her side. 'He's obviously a spy,' she snarled, 'and she's obviously his accomplice. He will disappear; she can audition for the Happiness Patrol. Take them both to the waiting zone.'

'What does that mean?' asked the Doctor.

'You're under arrest.'

'About time,' said Ace.

'Yes,' agreed the Doctor. 'We haven't got all night.'

They were marched at gunpoint through the gloomy streets. Ace's first impressions were confirmed. The city looked as if it had been built during a period of optimism, with bright colours and beautiful ornate buildings. But now it seemed as if there were neither the time nor the inclination to organize the upkeep of the streets. The paint was faded and peeling, and here and there an iron balcony or streetlamp had fallen down into the street and been left to accumulate dirt and rust.

They reached a quiet side-street lit by a single light. Under the light, incongruously, sat an old-fashioned one-armed bandit. A man, Harold V, was playing the machine, pulling at the arm but deriving no joy from it. On the ground, a few feet away from him, was an abandoned go-kart.

While Ace was taking in these things, a woman, wearing the familiar outfit of the Happiness Patrol, approached them. She was carrying a sweet-tray around her neck. With her uniform and her sweets, she reminded Ace of the usherettes at the Perivale Odeon. But Ace forgot the comparison when she saw the woman's face. Ace had never seen human eyes like these: instead of the glassy stare of an usherette there was the steely gaze of a predator – the ruthlessness of an eagle as it circles over a frightened rabbit. Ace watched as the woman accepted the cans of nitro-nine which Daisy K had removed from Ace when she had been searched.

'I thought we'd been arrested,' said Ace, as the Happiness Patrol withdrew, leaving them with the lugubrious man and the frightening woman, known to the Happiness Patrol as Priscilla P. 'I thought we were going to prison.' She turned to the Doctor but he was standing next to the one-armed bandit, offering advice.

'Hold the two bananas and nudge it. It never fails,' he said.

Ace, who knew a thing or two about one-armed bandits, watched with professional interest as Harold V followed the Doctor's instructions. Nothing happened.

'Ah well,' said Ace, smugly. 'You can't win them all.'

Harold V turned from the machine, his long face showing no sign of emotion. 'It's all right,' he said. 'I don't like winning.'

'Why's that?' asked the Doctor.

'First of all, I'm a killjoy,' Harold patiently explained, as he fed another token into the one-armed bandit. 'And second, I don't like the prize.'

'What is the prize?' Ace was interrupted by a tinny blast of electronic music coming frm the machine. Lights flashed, and as the fanfare came to an end, Helen A's smiling face appeared on a monitor set into the one-armed bandit. Harold V had won the jackpot. 'You're about to find out,' he said.

On the screen, Helen A's eyes sparkled, set off by her soft make-up, and her pink and mauve hair bounced gently. 'Congratulations and well played.' Her voice was soft. 'Here is your prize joke. Did you hear about the killjoy who won an outing with the Happiness Patrol?' She paused for effect. 'He was tickled to death! Enjoy yourself!'

The Doctor, Ace and Harold V watched in silence as the image of Helen A faded from the screen. Suddenly the machine erupted with tumultuous applause and canned laughter. After about fifteen seconds the noise stopped as abruptly as it had started.

The Doctor considered the jackpot prize. 'I see what you mean,' he said to Harold. 'Her delivery's terrible.'

'The joke's not much good either,' said Harold.

Again the Doctor had to agree. 'You're right. It's awful.

It's tasteless, smug, and worst of all, it's badly constructed. Who writes that stuff?'

'I wrote it,' said Harold.

'You wrote it?' Ace was amazed. She had never met anyone less funny than Harold V.

'I used to be her gag writer,' he explained, 'when I was Harold F. Then my brother disappeared. I went to look for him, and I heard of other disappearances. They caught me in the rocket-port zone trying to contact Terra Omega.' Harold V looked down at the ground remembering his desperate attempt at escape, remembering the triumph he had felt when he had contacted spies from Terra Omega, and the terror as he was hunted through the streets by the Happiness Patrol. Then there was the final humiliation when he was trapped. 'They brought me here, where I was regraded to Harold V.' He showed them the large 'V' sewn on to his tunic. Ace could see a few loose threads, presumably where the letter 'F' had been violently ripped off by Daisy K.

Something puzzled Ace. The way Harold V was talking, it sounded as if they were in prison. But looking around, there was nothing to keep them there. Priscilla P was still keeping a wary eye on them, but she looked benign, in spite of her chilling eyes. 'But what's keeping you here?' she asked Harold. 'Why don't we just stroll off?'

The Doctor had obviously been thinking along similar lines. He approached Priscilla P and doffed his hat. 'Excuse me,' he said.

Priscilla P snarled. 'Yes?'

The Doctor waved his hand around, taking in the street. 'Is this a prison?'

Priscilla P smiled, and almost appeared to laugh. 'A prison? Of course not. This is the waiting zone. There are no prisons on Terra Alpha – miserable places.'

The Doctor nodded. 'So there is no chance whatsoever that this is a place of incarceration, and we are free to go at any time.'

Ace watched this exchange from her position next to the

21

one-armed bandit. She noticed for the first time that their part of the street was marked off from the rest of the street by a thin line of tape. The Doctor walked purposefully toward the line.

Priscilla P watched him like a hawk. 'Well, yes and no. This isn't a prison,' she said. She delved in her sweet tray and produced a small handgun. 'But cross that line and you're a dead man.'

4

The balloons and bunting in the yard were not for a party –
they were for an execution. Helen A thought it was
unfortunate that Terra Alphans had to die if they refused
to enjoy themselves, but if it was unavoidable, which it
appeared to be, then she was determined that everybody
else would enjoy the occasion. So Daisy K was in high
spirits as she led Andrew X into the execution yard.

Andrew X was Harold V's brother. He was a writer, and
for many years he had written about oppression on Terra
Alpha. He knew that his work would never be published
while Helen A ruled the planet, but with the help of
Omegan secret agents, he had managed to smuggle his work
to nearby Terra Omega. After many long and bloody wars,
an uneasy truce had been signed between the two planets,
but many political commentators were now predicting that
hostilities would restart. Andrew X was something of a
celebrity on Terra Omega, although he had never been
there because his identity card had long been confiscated.
His books, written under a pseudonym, were always high
on the best-seller lists, and his poetry and articles were
always published anonymously in the weekly and monthly
Omegan magazines.

But Andrew X's success on Terra Omega was a time
bomb waiting to go off under his feet: an Alphan agent,
working undercover as a taxi pilot, had long been monitor-
ing his writings. Logging every reference to Terra Alpha,
she had worked for five years piecing together a description
of the area around Andrew X's home. Then Andrew X had

written a short poem about a beautiful old theatre that was being allowed to crumble away. When the taxi pilot read the poem she punched the air with joy: she knew the theatre well – she had grown up only two streets away from it. The poem was the final piece in the jigsaw, and she knew where Andrew X published from – his days of freedom were numbered.

The agent was well rewarded when she communicated her discoveries to Daisy K, and the Happiness Patrol were soon breaking down Andrew X's door. They burnt his manuscripts and smashed his printing presses. Andrew X came quietly. The arrival of the Happiness Patrol was no surprise to him – the only surprise was that it had taken them so long to find him.

He had been kept in solitary confinement for six months while he had been interrogated. But Helen A had finally grown bored of him, and his execution order was signed. By the time he stumbled into the execution yard, occasionally reaching out for support as he felt his legs giving way, he was starved and weak, his black clothes torn and dirty. Three members of the Happiness Patrol marched behind him, the seams of their costumes razor-sharp; at the end of the procession was Joseph C in full military regalia.

Andrew X was positioned in the middle of the yard, and the Happiness Patrol formed up to be inspected by Joseph C. He complimented each of them on their diligence and appearance and then reached Daisy K at the head of the line.

'Congratulations,' said Joseph C, shaking her warmly by the hand. Daisy K smiled her warmest smile, basking in his approval. Joseph C moved over to Andrew X, waiting quietly in the centre of the yard. He held out his hand. Andrew X was too weak to respond so Joseph C reached down and grasped Andrew X's limp hand.

'Bad luck, old man,' said Joseph C. 'Still, we've got to be fair, haven't we? Wouldn't be cricket, otherwise.'

Helen A sat in front of a monitor in the headquarters of

the Happiness Patrol observing these scenes with impatience. She was always the same watching executions – she wanted to dispense with the preliminaries and get on with the action. This feeling was particularly strong for the execution of Andrew X because she regarded him as the worst sort of killjoy – a traitor. Still, Joseph was always telling her that it was important to do things properly and that the preliminaries were a vital part of the execution process. She didn't often listen to Joseph, it was true, but he seemed to feel strongly about this, and she was prepared to make a concession.

Her viewing was interrupted by a soft tap on the door. She spun round in her chair to find the roly-poly figure of Gilbert M slipping into the room.

'You wanted to see me, ma'am.'

At first Helen A was puzzled, but then she remembered.

'Just idle curiosity, Gilbert M,' she said. 'I wondered what the Kandy Man has conjured up for us tonight.'

'It's a fondant surprise, ma'am,' said Gilbert M.

'Flavour?' she asked.

'Strawberry, ma'am,' said Gilbert.

Helen A licked her lips. 'Delicious,' she said, 'my favourite.'

In the waiting zone the Doctor was playing the one-armed bandit, trying to avoid winning the jackpot. Harold V was sitting slumped against the wall, giving Ace a list of all the things Helen A considered a crime against happiness.

'Dark clothes, as well,' he said. 'Overcoats, trilbies, shoes, wellington boots – if they're black, they're blacked, if you see what I mean.' Ace looked blank. 'They're proscribed.'

'Proscribed?' said Ace.

'Prohibited,' said the Doctor. He sat down beside Harold V. 'So you're telling us that Helen A punishes people for wearing dark clothes.'

Harold V nodded his assent. 'Public grief she calls it. It also covers listening to slow music.'

'Which explains that horrible lift music,' said Ace.

'And reading poems,' continued Harold V. 'Unless they're limericks, of course,' he said by way of an afterthought.

'But this is terrible,' said the Doctor, jumping up.

'Walking in the rain, as well,' said Harold V, 'if you're on your own and don't take an umbrella.'

Ace found all this hard to believe. 'But why don't people stand up to her?'

'Simple,' said Harold, 'people are scared.'

The Doctor recalled the fanatical grins of the Alphan militia. 'Remember the Happiness Patrol, Ace,' he said.

Ace looked defiant. 'A bunch of ratbags.'

By now the Doctor knew Ace well enough to know when to curb her enthusiasm for a fight. 'Ratbags with guns,' he said.

Harold V had pulled himself to his feet and was leaning against the wall. Before he spoke he made sure that Priscilla P was far enough away not to be able to hear.

'The Happiness Patrol is the nice side of her regime,' he said. 'Do you know who the Kandy Man is, Doctor?'

'He sounds like a sweetie!'

Harold V showed no sign of being amused. 'He's dangerous.'

'Dangerous?' said the Doctor, getting interested.

'He's doing experiments,' Harold explained. 'That's why we're here. He needs guinea pigs.' He turned to Ace, his face long and drawn. 'Guinea pigs like you and me,' he said lugubriously.

Ace was interested as well. 'What sort of experiments?' she asked.

Harold V shrugged and turned back to the one-armed bandit. 'I can't find out,' he said.

The Doctor, however, wouldn't let it rest. He needed every clue he could find to unravel the mystery of Terra Alpha. 'So what else does he do, this Kandy Man?'

Harold V pulled a strawberry sherbet out of his pocket

26

and casually tossed it to the Doctor. 'He makes sweets,' said Harold.

'Thank goodness,' said Ace, snatching the sweet from the Doctor. 'Food at last.' And before anyone could stop her she popped the sweet in her mouth. Harold and the Doctor waited anxiously for the verdict. 'Delicious,' said Ace. 'Got any more?'

'My last one,' said Harold, 'but there are plenty about. The Kandy Man makes thousands a day – gives them to the Happiness Patrol so that they can reward the happiest citizens.'

'He sounds an interesting sort of fellow, this Kandy Man,' said the Doctor. 'I shall look forward to meeting him.'

'So this Kandy Man,' said Ace, 'the one who makes the sweets, you reckon he is the one behind the disappearances – like the disappearance of your brother.'

'Oh yes,' said Harold. 'No question about it. But he's just one of them. There are different ways of disappearing on Terra Alpha.'

'Like what?' asked the Doctor.

'Essentially,' said Harold, 'there seem to be three main ways of disappearing. The late show at the Forum, a visit to the Kandy Kitchen, or . . .' Harold V paused and scratched his head. 'Or something else,' he said.

'What sort of something else?' asked Ace impatiently.

Harold V shook his head. 'I don't know exactly,' he said, 'but rumour has it that Helen A favours the firing squad.'

Harold's brother, Andrew X, was looking down the barrels of three Happiness Patrol fun guns. He, too, had heard the rumours about firing squads. He thought grimly that he wouldn't be around to be able to confirm them. He was only vaguely aware of Joseph C, who was reading from a long scroll.

'Oh dear, oh dear,' said Joseph C, looking sympathetically towards Andrew. 'I'm afraid it says here,' he said,

27

waving the scroll in the air, 'that you've been found guilty of an ostentatious display of public grief. Dear, dear, dear.'

It was all lies. When the Happiness Patrol had tracked him down, Andrew X had laughed in their faces.

He heard a click as the Happiness Patrol primed the fun guns. Joseph C reached into his pocket and pulled out a cap. Andrew noticed that it was a rather beautiful cap – a rainbow cap of many colours. As Joseph placed it on his head, Andrew was glad that this cap was one of the last things he would see on Terra Alpha

Joseph C continued his speech. 'You've been sentenced to the severest penalty decreed by Helen A.'

Andrew looked straight in front of him – straight at the guns. Then he closed his eyes and braced himself, waiting for the end.

'Patrol dismissed!' It was Daisy K. Andrew opened his eyes to see the guns being lowered and the Happiness Patrol marching out of the yard. Was it a reprieve?

Helen A always enjoyed the moment when the victim's hopes were raised. She was feeling better. Gilbert had brought her a box of her favourite truffles and she was chewing one contentedly. As she watched the bewildered Andrew X on the monitor her finger hovered over a red button on the console in front of her.

'What do you think, Gilbert M? Shall I push the button?'

Gilbert M stifled a yawn. 'Yes, ma'am. Whatever you think.'

Helen A slowly brought her finger down on the button.

The Kandy Man was behind with his weekly quota of sweets. He needed Gilbert M, and as usual Gilbert M was nowhere to be found. The Kandy Man was chopping strawberries and his anger was making him more violent and causing him to be more careless than usual. Thinking about Gilbert's absence, he brutally brought down his knife. It sliced through the intended strawberry but went on and cleanly severed his left thumb. The Kandy Man wearily put down the knife.

'Drat!' he shouted. This was all he needed – now, apart from everything else, he would have to spend time putting back his thumb. Getting it the right way round and matching nerve endings was a fiddly business.

He had just finished, and was picking up the knife to continue his work, when the smiling skull on the shelf next to him lit up and started flashing. The Kandy Man sighed and again put down the knife. Why did Helen A always choose the most inconvenient time for her executions? Why was he never consulted? He padded across the Kandy Kitchen, deliberately taking a little more time than necessary, and turned a small metal wheel one complete revolution. The Kandy Kitchen gradually came to life: other metal wheels turned, lights flashed and pipes creaked. Above it all there was the noise, a quiet trickling that grew into a great rushing sound. It howled around his ears, filling every corner of the Kandy Kitchen.

The Kandy Man sat down heavily, took a gingerbread man out of a nearby jar and bit off its head. He was having a hard day – he needed a break.

The noise was the first indication to Andrew X that something was happening in the execution yard. It was coming from deep inside the huge pipe suspended above his head and getting louder all the time – in seconds the sound was almost unbearable. Andrew X clasped his hands over his head. He saw Joseph C's benign smile and then he saw nothing as he was engulfed by thousands of gallons of a viscous red liquid pouring out of the pipe.

Joseph C was still smiling when Andrew X stopped moving, smothered by the sludge. 'The fondant surprise!' he said happily. He dipped his finger into the red liquid to taste it. 'Mmm,' he said, 'strawberry!'

5

Helen A turned off the monitor. She was satisfied: it was a job well done, and entertaining as well. She turned to Gilbert M and caught him yawning again.

He waved half-heartedly. 'Well, I must be going,' he said.

Helen A was annoyed with him. She felt he wasn't entering into the spirit of things. 'So soon,' she said. 'Aren't you forgetting something?'

Gilbert M looked blank.

'We haven't finished yet,' said Helen A. 'There's still his brother Harold V to deal with.'

'Ah, his brother.'

Helen A decided that Gilbert M needed to be reminded of a few priorities. 'Families are very important to people's happiness,' she said, smiling her most sincere smile.

But Gilbert M knew she was in a dangerous mood. He smiled back. 'Oh, I do agree,' he said quickly.

Helen A warmed to her theme. 'I'm a great believer in keeping families together.' She switched on the monitor, and they both watched Harold V playing the one-armed bandit in the waiting zone.

Harold V had told the Doctor and Ace everything he knew, and was now tired of talking. Priscilla P had noticed them whispering and had moved closer. The Doctor was getting restless: he looked at his watch.

'Time we were going, Professor?' asked Ace.

'We've got a night's work ahead of us,' agreed the Doctor, 'and I think we've learned enough.'

Ace leapt up. This was more like it! 'Ace!' she said. 'A prison break!'

'A waiting zone break,' the Doctor corrected her. 'And I think we'll take our new friend with us.'

Harold V looked up from the one-armed bandit. 'What's that?'

'We're going to escape,' whispered Ace.

Harold V's expression didn't change. 'There is no escape,' he said.

Watching the monitor Helen A could not hear this exchange, but she could see Harold V turning back to the one-armed bandit. She slammed her palm on to a button on the console.

Harold V pulled the lever.

The charge of electricity that passed through his body was so massive that he died instantly. Sparks flew from the one-armed bandit and a wisp of smoke escaped into the air.

Ace was first to reach to Harold V, but it was clear that it was too late. Priscilla P sauntered over and laughed quietly to herself. 'I think he got a buzz out of that,' she said.

Ace could control herself no longer. 'Shut up!' she cried and threw herself towards Priscilla P. Priscilla P's grip tightened on the trigger of her gun, but she had no need to use it, for the Doctor got to Ace first and held her back.

'Easy, Ace!' he said.

Priscilla P looked at Ace with contempt and then nodded towards the body of Harold V. 'Rather a shocking experience,' she laughed.

Ace struggled to free herself from the Doctor's grip. 'Let me get at her!' she screamed. 'Let me shut her up!'

The Doctor strengthened his grip and spoke quietly to her. 'Not now. Save the anger. Use it – use it later.' Ace relaxed. 'Right now I need you clear-headed,' he said. 'You're no good to me like this.'

He let Ace go. She was calm now, but still trembling. She turned away from Priscilla P.

'I want to nail those scumbags,' she said to the Doctor. 'I want to make them very, very unhappy.'

'Don't worry, Ace,' said the Doctor softly. 'We will.'

Ace's hands were steady again by the time the Happiness Patrol guards arrived to remove Harold V's body. They slung him roughly into a body bag and hauled it into their jeep. The Doctor could see that Ace needed distracting – another outburst could cost their lives. He led Ace over to the abandoned go-kart.

'What do you think?' he said.

'Booby-trapped,' said Ace. 'No question.'

The Doctor turned to Priscilla P, who was following their every move with her fun gun.

'Tell me, Priscilla P,' he said.

'Yes,' she replied politely.

'I was wondering about your go-kart,' said the Doctor, gesturing with the tip of his umbrella.

'Not my go-kart,' said Priscilla P. 'The waiting zone go-kart.'

'But where did it come from?'

'I think it belonged to some killjoy brought here by the Happiness Patrol. But it's all right – he doesn't need it any more.'

The Doctor flicked a speck of dirt off the go-kart's bumper. 'So if my friend and I were to get into it and drive off, what would you do?'

'Nothing,' said Priscilla P.

'Nothing?'

Priscilla P gave the Doctor her most charming smile. 'Absolutely nothing.'

The Doctor feigned surprise. 'You wouldn't raise the alarm, shoot us, or order a missile strike from low orbit?'

Priscilla P looked horrified at the suggestion. 'I told you, Doctor. I would do nothing.'

The Doctor went back to Ace who was peering into the go-kart, trying to identify the components of a Terra

Alphan engine. 'You're right,' the Doctor told her. 'It is booby-trapped.'

Something was obviously worrying Priscilla P. The longer the Doctor and Ace spent examining the go-kart, the jumpier she seemed to get. She was now right at the far side of the waiting zone, as far away from them as possible.

'What are you doing?' she called, trying to disguise the anxiety in her voice.

It was the Doctor's turn to play innocent. 'Nothing,' he cried, giving Priscilla P a little wave.

This did not seem to allay her fears. She could now see Ace fiddling with the controls, examining the ignition. 'You're not thinking of starting that?' she asked, trying to sound as unconcerned as possible.

'No,' said Ace, continuing her work on the ignition.

Priscilla P knew her duty. She had worked for many years in the Happiness Patrol, mostly on night patrols. And although she regarded waiting zone duty as demeaning to one of her experience in the field, she knew she had been entrusted with two high-category prisoners. But she also realized that every so often a moment arrived when duty had to come second to self-preservation. Watching the Doctor and the foolish girl tampering with the go-kart, she knew that moment had arrived. She edged away from them, slowly at first, crossing the line of the waiting zone. She checked one last time. 'You're sure you're not thinking of starting that, Doctor?'

'Positive,' said the Doctor.

That was enough for Priscilla P. She didn't trust the strange man with the straw hat and umbrella – she was going. She bolted round the corner, away from the waiting zone, ran down a long arcade, and dived into a recessed alcove, dimly lit by a single ancient ornate lamp. She crouched, covered her ears, and waited for the explosion.

The Doctor had extricated a bomb from under the go-kart and was wondering what to do with it. It was a situation he had been in before, but one that he never relished. Ace wasn't helping. She was now sitting in the

33

driver's seat of the go-kart, impatiently drumming her fingers on the wheel.

'Here,' she said. 'Give it to me.'

The Doctor tried to concentrate on the job in hand. 'Get off,' he said.

But Ace wouldn't go away. 'It's a bomb, isn't it?'

'Ace, I'm trying to defuse it.'

'Let me have a go.'

The Doctor had spotted the detonator. He started to remove it. 'I'm trying not to blow us both to pieces.'

Ace started sulking. 'I never get to have any fun.'

Working very carefully, the Doctor completed the delicate operation. 'Start the go-kart, Ace. You can drive.' He vaulted into the passenger seat as the machine exploded into life. The tyres screeched as they took a sharp left. The go-kart roared past a long stone arcade.

'Look!' shouted the Doctor, trying to make himself heard above the din. Ace turned her head just in time to see the amazed expression on Priscilla P's face as they raced past the alcove where she was still waiting for the explosion. She leapt up from her hiding place, a hand fumbling for her fun gun. By the time she was in the street firing after the go-kart, Ace and the Doctor were well out of her range.

Priscilla P heard a noise behind her, and spun round on the balls of her feet, the fun gun primed for use. But it was only Susan Q, her subordinate in the Happiness Patrol.

'Priscilla,' said Susan, 'I hope I haven't caught you at a bad time.'

There was no love lost between Priscilla and Susan. 'What do you want?' barked Priscilla.

'I was supposed to be collecting one of the prisoners for the Happiness Patrol auditions,' said Susan.

Susan had broken one of the unspoken rules of Terra Alpha, and Priscilla was quick to put her right. 'We don't have any prisoners on Terra Alpha. We don't have any prisons and we don't have any prisoners.'

Susan gazed after the Doctor and Ace, who were disappearing round a corner in the distance. 'Well, we certainly don't have any now, do we?'

6

Helen A, relaxing in her suite of rooms, took the news of Ace and the Doctor's escape badly. At times like this – times of great disappointment in those on whom she had conferred responsibility – she always found consolation in the same way. She crossed the room to the large gilded cage in the corner and gently lifted the embroidered sheet to reveal the only creature who never let her down, her Fifi.

Fifi was of a species indigenous to Terra Alpha. A small, ferocious, dog-like creature with a row of sharp dorsal spikes which flicked into an upright position when she was alert. Her body was covered with a scraggy wispy fur and her eyes glowed like a cat's. For years Fifi's species had been considered impossible to train by the Earth settlers on Terra Alpha and had been hunted for sport. The walls of many wealthy Alphan homes were adorned with the tails of Fifi's ancestors. This had continued until a few years ago, when the species had been wiped out – all except Fifi.

Helen A led a special expedition to the interior to hunt down the last of these vicious predators. After many weeks of searching, Fifi was located in the foothills of the mountains of Claffam. Helen A always left her party and hunted alone; she was many miles away from the others when she came face to face with Fifi on a rocky escarpment.

They liked each other immediately.

Several hours later, long after all the other hunters had returned to camp, Helen A arrived, with Fifi trotting obediently at her heels.

Since that day, they had remained fiercely loyal to each

other. Fifi retained her hostility to everything else, but would do anything to please Helen A. Similarly, Helen A turned to Fifi at times of crisis. She loved to indulge Fifi, and now slipped some chocolate truffles into her cage. Fifi growled contentedly.

This idyllic scene was interrupted by a sharp knock at the door. Helen A replaced the embroidered sheet over the cage and opened the door to Daisy K. She motioned to a chair, carved after an original found in the ashes at Versailles after the bomb, and Daisy K sat down. Helen A knew that Daisy K had not been at the waiting zone at the time of the escape, but Daisy K had been the officer in charge of the relevant sector of the city, and as such the break-out was ultimately her responsibility.

Helen A pretended she had not been told of the escape. 'I understand that you arrested an alien spy earlier.'

Daisy K took a deep breath. 'Yes, but he's just disappeared.'

'Excellent,' said Helen A. She approved of disappearances.

'You don't understand,' said Daisy.

'I don't understand?'

'I mean he's vanished.'

Helen A smiled at her. She decided to make Daisy K squirm. 'Well, as long as he's disappeared.'

'He hasn't actually disappeared – he's vanished,' said Daisy K. 'He'll disappear as soon as we can find him.' She waited for the explosion. But Helen A sounded calm.

'Do you mean to say that not only has he not disappeared, he's also escaped?'

Daisy K tried to sound confident. 'As soon as we find him, he'll disappear.'

Helen A's voice dropped, almost to a whisper. 'It's been a long night, Daisy K,' she said. 'Don't let me down.'

The engine of the go-kart was purring like a cat as Ace and the Doctor sped through the dimly lit streets of the capital of Terra Alpha. They had put some distance between themselves and the Happiness Patrol, and could no longer hear the wail of the pursuing sirens.

'Nothing like a nice quiet night, eh, Ace?' said the Doctor.

'Yeah,' said Ace as they screamed round a corner. 'It's about time we had a rest.' But just as she was finishing her sentence, the engine started spluttering. Ace slammed her foot down, but the go-kart glided gently to a halt.

Half an hour later the Doctor's feet were still sticking out from under the go-kart as he tried to find out what was wrong with the engine. They had been hearing the sirens for about five minutes now, getting louder as the Happiness Patrol hunted them down. Ace was keeping a look-out from a street corner when she saw a patrol on foot turning over rubbish and looking into doorways. She recognized Daisy K from earlier in the evening.

She ran back to the go-kart and the Doctor. 'Any luck, Professor?' she asked his feet.

The Doctor did not appear from under the machine. 'I need a little more time.'

Ace took her decision. 'You've got it,' she said, and ran back to the corner. She put her fingers to her mouth and blew.

The Happiness Patrol stopped searching when they heard the piercing whistle. Daisy K looked up from the smelly pile of rubbish she was wading through to see Ace calmly walking down the street towards her.

'Oi!' shouted Ace, just in case they hadn't seen her.

Daisy K levelled her fun gun at Ace. 'I arrest you for the evasion of Happiness Patrol auditions,' she said.

Ace shrugged. 'Where are they?'

Daisy K suspected more insolence – she didn't like this cocky girl in her leather jacket. 'What do you mean?'

'I'm ready for your auditions,' said Ace. 'The question is, are they ready for me?'

Daisy K snapped her fingers and within a few moments Susan Q was at her side. 'Take her back to headquarters,' she barked. 'We'll continue the search for the spy.'

Ace was already being marched away by Susan Q when the Doctor finished his work on the go-kart engine and it spluttered back into life. 'That should do it, Ace,' he said as he scrambled out from underneath the machine. 'Nice of the Happiness Patrol to leave us in peace.'

Pulling himself to his feet, he saw that he was alone. 'Ace?' he called hopefully, but he knew that she would already be involved – she would be embracing the danger with every ounce of that huge heart.

The Doctor sighed as he jumped into the driver's seat of the go-kart and slipped the vehicle into gear. He was not a moment too soon, for Happiness Patrol guards raced round a corner and opened fire just as he started moving. The Doctor weaved across the road to give them a harder target. He felt the machine jolt under him as a bullet ricocheted away, but there was no damage and he screeched round the corner to safety.

A few streets away Earl Sigma heard the sounds of gunfire and took his harmonica from his lips. But gunfire on Terra Alpha was not a strange sound to anyone who had been there for more than a couple of days, and soon he was playing again as he walked along. A slow, plangent, haunting melody, ripped from the deepest recesses of his soul and released into the thick black air of the Terra Alphan night.

But Earl was being watched. As he walked by, a manhole cover was quietly slid to one side, and bright eyes watched in the darkness. The cover was replaced when he was out of earshot, but another was opened as he walked down the next street. This time there were four, eight, sixteen eyes, all watching his progress – watching and waiting.

Ace could feel the nozzle of Susan Q's fun gun in her back as they walked through the streets heading back towards the centre of Terra Alpha.

'What's your name, then?' she asked. 'Valerie V, Zelda Z. Wendy W . . .'

She felt a stab of pain as the gun was jabbed in her back.

'Quiet!' ordered Susan Q. She motioned to Ace to stop walking.

Susan Q held a finger to her lips. And then Ace understood why they had stopped – to listen to the music! They could just hear the faint strains of Earl's harmonica floating across the rooftops. The music was beautiful, but sad, so sad . . .

'Do you hear the music?' Susan Q spoke softly.

'He sounds sad,' said Ace. 'If it's a he.'

'Yes, he does.'

Ace's anger erupted. 'So you want to arrest him, put him in jail, shoot him . . .'

But Susan Q was different from the other members of the Happiness Patrol that Ace had come across. Ace could see that she cared about this music.

'I just want to listen to him' said Susan Q.

Ace still couldn't quite believe her. 'Oh yeah?' she said, unable to keep the sarcasm out of her voice.

Susan Q paused for a moment as if she were carefully considering what to say next. Then she looked into Ace's eyes and spoke.

'I like it,' she said. 'I used to have a collection of blues seventy-eights that came from old Earth. I had to destroy them when I was vetted for the Happiness Patrol – all except one.'

Ace listened carefully. She knew that Susan Q, by confiding in her, was taking a great risk.

'*Lucille*,' said Susan Q, 'sung by Big Joe Turner.'

'And you managed to hide it from them?'

'No. They found it.'

'Oh dear,' said Ace. She had seen enough of the Happiness Patrol to know the danger that Susan Q could find herself in. She also realized that Susan Q was on the point of defecting. What other reason could there be for these revelations?

Susan Q held out her hand. 'Susan Q,' she said.

Ace was distracted. 'What?' she said.

39

'My name. It used to be Susan L before I was demoted.'

'But you're all right? They haven't done anything to you?'

'No,' said Susan Q with a wry smile. 'Not yet.'

The Doctor, heading towards the centre of the town, was the only one who couldn't hear the blues tune. He was concentrating too hard on the unhealthy sounds from the go-kart's engine. It had been coughing a bit, and now it was misfiring. As the go-kart went slower and slower and it became clear that he would have to give it another examination, he looked round for help.

The streets were deserted.

The auditions for the Happiness Patrol were a weekly event in the city. The candidates were usually girls from the towns and villages in the remote parts of the planet, captured by the press-gangs sent out regularly from the city. Helen A reasoned that if the Happiness Patrol were to lose members to the guerrilla tactics of dissidents in these parts of the planet, then it was only fair if the gaps in the patrol's ranks were plugged by the guerrillas' own people.

The auditions took the form of a variety show. The Happiness Patrol was the most obviously visible side of Helen A's regime and she wanted its members to be positive, gutsy and talented – she wanted them to have star quality. Helen A long ago decided that the best way to assess these qualities was to ask the candidates to present a variety turn to her in the Forum. It didn't matter what it was – a dance, a song, a piece of magic, or a stand-up comedy routine. All that Helen A asked was that she felt better at the end of the act, that she left the theatre with a smile on her face. Those who succeeded went on to join the Happiness Patrol; those who didn't were never heard of again.

Susan Q, prior to being press-ganged into the Happiness Patrol, had worked as a singer and dancer in theatres all over Terra Alpha. She passed the Happiness Patrol audition with the highest ever marks and, among her other duties, was quickly put to work coaching the candidates for the auditions.

She was now standing in a large room in the headquarters of the Happiness Patrol watching Ace trying to twirl a baton over her head. It was terrible.

'OK, Ace,' said Susan Q, as kindly as possible, 'stop there. I can't take any more. We won't even bother looking at your dancing.' She racked her brains for something Ace might be good at. 'Do you know any jokes?'

Ace shook her head. 'I always forget jokes.'

'How about songs?'

Ace remembered an old song from the 1950s. She thought it might be American. It had always been one of her favourites. 'I know this great song about this guy and his girlfriend. She drops the ring he gave her on a railway track, and when she goes back to get it she's killed by a train, so he's really miserable for the rest of his life. It's fantastic.'

Susan Q was exasperated. 'Happy songs, Ace,' she exclaimed. 'Songs about sunshine and furry animals.'

They went through a few other ideas: juggling, card tricks, and even tightrope walking. None of it was any good.

Susan Q was tired. She could see through the charade – could see the pointlessness of it all. She told Ace to take a breather.

They both sat on the floor, and Susan Q stared into space. 'You know, Ace . . .'

'Yeah?'

'I woke up one morning . . .'

'I know that song,' said Ace enthusiastically.

Susan Q laughed. 'There are a million blues songs that start like that. But I did.'

Ace looked puzzled.

'I did wake up one morning and suddenly something was very clear. I couldn't go on smiling. Smiling while my friends disappeared. Wearing this uniform. Smiling and trying to pretend I'm someone I'm not. Trying to pretend

41

I'm happy. Better to let it end. Better just to relax and let it happen. I woke up one morning and realized it was all over.'

There was a long silence after Susan Q finished talking. Then Ace moved over to her and laid a hand gently on Susan Q's arm. 'Look,' she said, 'I'm sorry.'

Susan Q shook her head. None of it was Ace's fault. 'I think we'll abandon our rehearsal.'

Ace was relieved. She didn't know what would happen to her now but she certainly didn't want to go through with the farce of a Happiness Patrol audition. 'I'm not Happiness Patrol material anyway,' she said proudly. 'They stand for everything I hate. Like you said, smiling all the time – smiling when it doesn't mean anything. I'm not one of them: I can't twirl a baton; I can't dance; I can't sing.'

Susan Q appreciated the speech. But when she turned to look at Ace the expression on her face was deadly serious. 'No,' she said, 'but there is one thing you might be very good at.'

'Oh yeah?'

'Yes. A disappearing act.'

Ace was intrigued. 'What do I have to do?'

Susan Q produced a key from a small purse and held it out to Ace. 'It's simple,' she said. 'I close my eyes. When I open them you're gone.'

Ace did not need a second invitation. Within moments she was through the door and into the blackness of the night.

The ailing go-kart had rolled to a halt next to a bench beneath a streetlight. The Doctor climbed wearily under the machine. He was fed up with Alphan engineering. The Doctor, however, was being watched. Silas P sidled out from the shadows and sat down on the bench. He took out his copy of *The Grief* and started to read.

The Doctor was making no progress. He hauled himself out from under the go-kart and found himself staring at the back of Silas P's newspaper. 'Excuse me,' said the Doctor.

42

Silas P scented his forty-eighth scalp – Helen A would be delighted. He put down his paper and raised his hat.

'You wouldn't have a small automotive jack, would you?' asked the Doctor amiably.

'I'm afraid not,' said Silas, proffering his hand, which was accepted by the Doctor. 'But I can offer you the hand of friendship. Sit down. Tell me about yourself.'

The Doctor had all but decided to give up with the go-kart. He needed to get back to the heart of the danger, especially if Ace was in trouble. Perhaps the man in the hat would be able to give him some answers.

He sat down on the bench, next to Silas P. 'I'm looking for Helen A,' he said. 'Perhaps you could point me in the right direction.'

'I can tell you where to find her,' said Silas P. 'But make sure you're smiling when you meet her.'

'Smiling?'

'She hates miserable people. Haven't you heard about the massacre?'

The Doctor remembered Harold V mentioning a massacre, shortly before his death. 'I've heard rumours,' he said.

'Helen A got angry at the end of last year. She sent out her spies to find the most depressing township on the planet. The Happiness Patrol went in and razed the place to the ground.'

The Doctor could barely suppress his anger. He was beginning to understand fully the extent of the evil abroad on Terra Alpha. 'But why?' he cried.

'Policy,' said Silas P. He saw the look in the Doctor's eyes. 'I'm sorry, I didn't mean to distress you.'

'I'm not distressed,' said the Doctor. 'I'm angry. Why do the people let her walk all over them?'

Silas P sighed. He liked this bit of his act best. The bit when he laid the blame on his superiors. 'There are lots of reasons. The Happiness Patrol, the Kandy Man . . .'

The Doctor interrupted him. 'The Kandy Man! He's next on my list of people to see.'

Silas P looked concerned. 'Then I'd cross him off fast if

43

I were you. He's Helen A's henchman – does all her dirty work.' He paused for effect. 'There are small pockets of resistance, though. Quiet murmurings of rebellion. Are you interested?'

'But of course,' said the Doctor.

Silas P looked furtively from side to side and then over his shoulder. His voice dropped to a whisper. 'There's a place, a secret place, where we're planning for the day when Helen A and the Kandy Man will be called to account.' He produced something from inside his raincoat. 'Here – my card.'

'Thanks.' The Doctor read the legend. 'Silas P.'

'Other side.'

'Happiness Patrol undercover.' The Doctor was delighted. 'Excellent! Perhaps you could take a message . . .'

But Silas P didn't hear. He was blowing his whistle long and loud to summon members of the Happiness Patrol from all over the city to come and finish off this strange killjoy with the straw hat and umbrella.

Earl Sigma, observing the scene from the shadows, made his move. The harmonica spun out of his hand as he hit Silas P cleanly on the back of his head. The whistle flew from Silas's mouth.

The Doctor scooped up the harmonica and handed it back to Earl. 'Are you a musician?' he asked.

'Sort of,' said Earl, pocketing the instrument. They heard the first sirens of the Happiness Patrol.

'Shall we go?' asked the Doctor.

Silas P regained consciousness as Earl and the Doctor escaped down the street. He rubbed his head and looked around, trying to remember where he was and what had happened. He touched the cut on his head and his face contorted in pain. When he opened his eyes he looked down the barrels of five Happiness Patrol guns.

The Happiness Patrol guards had heard his whistle and hurried to this lonely spot. They had found this man in a trilby, obviously unhappy. That was enough.

'No!' screamed Silas P. 'Wait!'

But it was too late. The Happiness Patrol opened fire.

Earl Sigma and the Doctor were crouching in a doorway, trying to dodge the searchlights attached to the front of the Happiness Patrol jeeps. The shooting seemed to be dying down. The Doctor doffed his hat. 'I'm the Doctor,' he said.

'Earl Sigma,' said Earl.

'A sort of musician?'

'I'm actually a medical student,' explained Earl. 'Fifth year post med psychology.'

Something was puzzling the Doctor. 'Tell me,' he said, 'what does the Sigma mean?'

'It stands for alien. All visitors to Terra Alpha are called Sigma.'

'So you're travelling through the colonies?'

'Yeah,' said Earl. 'I'm on vacation, paying my way with music. But I kind of got stuck here.'

The Doctor understood why. 'Yes,' he said. 'Rather a fascinating planet from a psychological standpoint.'

The seachlights were getting brighter; the sound of the Happiness Patrol sirens louder. 'Let's go,' shouted Earl, leaping to his feet.

'Wait!' said the Doctor, holding Earl back. He had just noticed the sign above the doorway. Twelve extravagant, baroque letters which spelt Kandy Kitchen. He steered Earl through the door, which opened easily. 'In here,' he said. 'There's someone I'd like to meet.'

Inside, a steep staircase led down into the kitchen. At the bottom, Earl stared in amazement at the huge black pots on the stoves and their brightly coloured bubbling ingredients. The Doctor was examining the chopped ingredients laid out on the enormous wooden table.

'What is this place?' asked Earl, noticing the great wheels and cogs slowly revolving high up near the ceiling.

The Doctor looked grim. 'I believe it's where they make sweets.'

They were taken completely by surprise when Gilbert M

bustled in, chattering angrily to himself. The Doctor grabbed Earl Sigma and they dived underneath the table.

Gilbert M had seen them but was unconcerned. In truth he was rather grateful to have someone to listen to his catalogue of complaints. 'They think it's easy,' he moaned as he pottered around the kitchen. 'A thousand pounds of praline cracknel indeed!' He stirred one of the pots. 'They don't know about his moods.' He took the wooden spoon and tasted the mixture. 'He's terrible when he's roused.' He started shovelling ingredients into the pot. 'I tell them but they don't believe me.' He slammed the spoon down on the table. 'They're lucky they get any sweets at all.'

Gilbert M suddenly stopped talking. In the silence, Earl and the Doctor could hear strange sucking noises. The Doctor was reminded of his time in Peru with the Incas, and the sound of leeches being pulled from human skin. But this was the sound of the Kandy Man's feet sticking to floor as he lumbered into the Kandy Kitchen. He was carrying a large hammer.

He had heard Gilbert M's prattle and was annoyed. 'Enough!' he bellowed. Gilbert M scurried into the corner and the Doctor and Earl Sigma retreated further under the table.

'Where are my specimens?' the Kandy Man asked, brandishing his hammer.

But even this wouldn't deflect Gilbert M from his theme. 'If they think it's so easy they should have a go at making sweets themselves. Most of them wouldn't know popcorn from peppermints,' he added, by way of a last word on the matter.

The Kandy Man managed to control himself. He tried to be reasonable. 'I said where are my specimens. It's time for an experiment.'

Gilbert M decided to be co-operative. 'I think they just nipped under the table,' he said.

'What do we do?' whispered Earl.

'Follow me,' said the Doctor.

The sucking noises were getting louder as the Kandy

Man approached the table. Just as he was bending down to look under it the Doctor, closely followed by Earl, slipped out and headed for one of the ovens. They took cover behind it.

'There's no one here,' said the Kandy Man, summoning up all his reserves of patience.

Gilbert M scratched his head. 'But I saw them. We had a bit of a chat. They seemed very pleasant.'

The Kandy Man gritted his teeth. 'Show me,' he said.

The Doctor and Earl were watching the scene from behind the oven. 'I thought you said you wanted to meet him?' said Earl.

The Doctor had changed his mind. 'Another time perhaps. At the moment things are looking a bit sticky.' The Doctor glanced around the Kandy Kitchen. They were near the stairs leading to street level. 'We'll try for the door,' he said.

Gilbert M was under the table, scratching his head. 'Well I'll be blowed. I could have sworn they were under here.'

The Kandy Man had had just about enough of this ridiculous charade. It was all Gilbert's fault, as usual. 'I can feel one of my moods coming on,' he growled.

The Doctor judged that this was the moment for them to make their break. 'Go!' he whispered, shoving Earl towards the stairs.

But the Kandy Man had seen them. He flicked a switch near his hand and an ornamental metal grille slammed down in front of the Doctor and Earl, barring their escape. As they struggled with the bars in vain, the Kandy Man sauntered over to them, his feet popping and squelching as he moved.

'Welcome to the Kandy Kitchen, gentlemen,' he said pleasantly.

The Doctor raised his hat. 'I'm sure the pleasure will be ours,' he said.

'I do hope so,' replied the Kandy Man. 'I like my volunteers to die with smiles on their faces.'

47

He threw back his head and laughed. His teeth were black.

If the Doctor and Earl had escaped to the street they would have found Ace, who was on the run from the Happiness Patrol. But she was heading away from the Kandy Kitchen. She paused for breath, only to find herself looking at a huge poster announcing:

TONIGHT – THE GRAND HAPPINESS PATROL AUDITION

but she ran on, listening to the sporadic rounds of machine-gun fire in the distance. Then a voice close behind her called: 'Halt, or I fire!'

Ace continued to run, gasping for breath. But now the machine-gun fire was much closer – a series of small explosions, almost inside her head. She dropped to the ground for cover. Then there was silence. She quickly looked around, saw nobody, and started running again. Down this street, up that street, down some steps, through an archway, round a corner – straight into Daisy K and her smoking fun gun.

Ace was beaten.

Daisy K said nothing. She just waited and watched as her guards joined her and slipped the handcuffs over Ace's wrists.

The Kandy Man was closing in on Earl and the Doctor when he was distracted by Gilbert M, who was fussing over the stove. 'It's boiling over, Kandy Man,' he said.

'Not now, Gilbert M!'

'But the pan's boiling over.'

'Ruins the flavour,' offered the Doctor.

The Kandy Man turned slowly and looked at the stove. He glared at Gilbert M. 'It's not my pan,' he said softly. 'It's one of your pans.'

The Doctor had seen a way out. There was a manhole cover only a few feet away. While Kandy Man and Gilbert

M were distracted by their argument, he started to move towards it. He gestured to Earl to follow him.

'It's one of your special non-stick pans,' said Gilbert M.

The Doctor eased off the manhole cover.

The Kandy Man's lip was twitching. 'Can't you see I'm busy?'

'But it's sticking,' said Gilbert M.

The Doctor dropped down from the Kandy Kitchen into the pipes. 'What charming people, eh, Earl?' No reply. 'Earl?' But Earl was not following him. The Doctor hauled himself back up into the Kitchen. Earl had not followed him because Earl was otherwise occupied. He was being strapped into a reclining chair by the Kandy Man, who seemed genuinely pleased to see the reappearance of the Doctor.

'You've come back to the scene of my crimes,' he smiled.

'I've come back for my friend,' said the Doctor.

The Kandy Man tightened the straps round Earl's arms and chest. 'It's very simple: your friend is going to die. Feel free to join him.' The Kandy Man waved at an identical reclining chair, next to Earl's. Gilbert M was waiting to help with the straps.

Fifi was purring softly, as Helen A ruffled the fur behind the creature's ears. Ace was horrified. She had never seen a creature quite like Fifi before, but she certainly wouldn't touch her. She was reminded of the scavenging dogs of Perivale, which she would watch in the early hours of the morning as they fought over the contents of a filthy dustbin.

Helen A planted a kiss on the top of Fifi's head and spoke to Ace. 'But we were so looking forward to your performance.' She tickled Fifi under her chin. 'Weren't we, Fifi?'

Ace was defiant. 'I didn't feel like it.'

Helen A looked as if she couldn't believe it. 'You didn't feel like auditioning for the Happiness Patrol? You didn't feel like dancing?'

The more Helen A smiled, the more Ace wanted to make her angry. 'I hate dancing,' she said.

But Helen A was again preoccupied with Fifi. 'Well, Fifi,' she cooed, 'what are we going to do about Ace Sigma?'

In a flash Fifi bared her teeth and lunged for Ace's throat. Ace recoiled straight into the nozzle of a Happiness Patrol guard's fun gun. Fifi still snapped and drooled, but now Ace could see the leash digging into the creature's neck. Helen A had decided to let Ace survive, at least for the moment. She closed her hand around Fifi's jaw and suddenly the creature was calm again, enjoying the soft touch of Helen A's hand on its scraggy fur.

Helen A smiled at Ace. 'You mustn't worry about Fifi,' she said. 'She's only being friendly.' She gave Fifi a chocolate. 'Aren't you my darling?'

Helen A glanced up at Ace, sharp now, harder than before. 'You're from one of the other planets, aren't you, Ace Sigma?'

Ace didn't know what she was talking about. 'I'm from Earth.'

Fifi growled softly.

'You're from Omega or Beta,' continued Helen A, 'your mission to spread discontent and dissension. Well, it won't work, Ace Sigma.'

Ace said nothing, happy to see the rising fury in Helen A.

Helen A detested the girl's insolent expression. 'My people are happy. They don't know the meaning of misery or despair, and as long as I'm in charge, I'll make sure they never do.'

There was a knock at the door.

The clouds lifted from Helen A's brow as she cried out cheerily in a sing-song voice. 'Happiness will prevail! Come in if you're happy!'

Daisy K dragged in Susan Q by the hair and threw her to the floor.

'Excellent!' said Helen A. 'Where did you find her?'

'She was hiding in a doorway at the Forum.'

Susan Q started to pull herself to her feet. Helen A fixed her with her gaze. 'You were hiding.' She thought for a moment. 'So you were unhappy about something?'

Susan Q knew this was a trap. 'No,' she said.

Helen A persisted. 'You were unhappy that Ace Sigma had been caught.'

'No.'

Helen A was enjoying the game. 'But you helped her to escape.'

'No!' screamed Susan Q. She had suffered a beating at the hands of Daisy K and her guards. She clutched her stomach and fell to the ground. Daisy K grabbed her hair again.

Ace reached breaking point. 'Why don't you leave her alone, face-ache?'

Helen A remained calm. 'Take Ace Sigma away, Daisy K.'

Daisy K threw Susan Q back down and twisted Ace's arm behind her back. 'To death row?'

'Not yet,' said Helen A. 'I haven't finished with her. But for the moment I'm more interested in this miserable creature.' She peered down at Susan Q.

Susan Q was adamant. 'I'm not miserable!'

Helen A inspected her nails. 'I think she's worked out that while she's still happy she's not breaking any laws.'

Dasy K nodded sycophantically.

'But there's a simple solution to that, isn't there, Daisy K?'

'Very simple,' Daisy K smiled.

Helen A went back to stroking Fifi. 'We make her unhappy.'

Fifi growled in eager anticipation.

The Doctor, now securely fastened into the second reclining chair, watched in fascination as the Kandy Man supervised Gilbert M, who was pouring different coloured liquids from bottles into test-tubes. Seldom had the Doctor seen such concentration.

51

The Kandy Man was giving Gilbert M his instructions. 'Twenty-five millilitres of caramel extract.' Gilbert selected another bottle and poured. 'And fifteen millilitres of the new formula vanilla essence.'

Earl was apprehensive. 'What's going on, Doctor?' he asked, struggling against the restraining straps.

If the Doctor moved very slowly he could manage to turn his head far enough to see Earl. 'I think the chef is trying out a new dish.'

The Kandy Man heard them talking, and left Gilbert to his work with the test-tubes. 'Comfortable, gentlemen?'

'We're still waiting for the hors-d'oeuvre,' said the Doctor. 'We haven't got all night.'

But the Kandy Man did not rise to the bait. 'Believe me, Doctor,' he said quietly. 'It's worth waiting for.' Gilbert M gave him two test-tubes. 'Temperature?' asked the Kandy Man.

'Fifty-eight degrees.'

'Thank you, Gilbert.' It seemed that they had got over their earlier disagreement. The Kandy Man turned back to the Doctor and Earl, strapped into the dentist's chairs. 'This is where you come in, gentlemen. The interesting part – the tasting.'

The mixture, whatever it was, smelt very good. The Doctor was intrigued. 'May we ask what it is?'

The Kandy Man was sniffing the concoction. He smiled his satisfaction. 'A labour of love, Doctor, a labour of love.'

This didn't tally with Harold V's description of the Kandy Man. 'Really,' said the Doctor. 'I didn't know you were the caring type.'

The Doctor had touched a raw nerve, and the Kandy Man sounded genuinely hurt. 'Just because Helen A prefers my ugly side, that doesn't mean I don't care,' he protested. 'Does it, Gilbert M?'

Gilbert M, busy with some strawberries, did not answer.

The Kandy Man hated being ignored. He erupted in fury. 'Gilbert M!'

Gilbert M casually looked up from the strawberries. 'No, no, of course not.'

He seemed unconcerned with the Kandy Man's tantrum.

But the Kandy Man was calm again. 'Thank you, Gilbert M,' he said politely. He turned back to the Doctor. 'And just because Helen A employs me as her executioner that doesn't mean I can't be creative.'

Earl had heard only one word. 'Executioner?'

The Kandy Man reassured him. 'No need to worry.' He held the test-tubes up to the light. 'Today you see before you the artistic, sensitive side of me. You see,' he said, glancing proudly at his kitchen, 'I make sweets. But not just any old sweets – sweets that are so good, so delicious, that sometimes the human frame is not equipped to bear the pleasure. Tell them what I'm trying to say, Gilbert M.'

Gilbert M sounded bored, as if he had heard it all before. 'He makes sweets that kill people.'

The Kandy Man had poured some of the mixture from a test-tube on to a small silver spoon. He held the spoon to Earl's lips. 'I think we'll start with you,' he said.

7

Terra Alpha was rich in sugar beet. Before the arrival of the colonists, several generations before, it had been allowed to grow wild, supporting most of the planet's indigenous species. But the ancestors of Helen A had quickly seen the commercial possibilities of harvesting the crop, particularly because no sugar grew on any of the other colony planets.

They had built huge grey factories in the flatlands to process the sugar. There was no concession to fun or jollity here. They were well away from the cities and out of the public gaze. The factories were utilitarian, designed for profit and no more. Captured dissidents provided the workforce, and they lived in drab prefabricated dwellings hastily constructed on the factory compounds. Known as drones, these men and women were not prisoners, but were banned from most parts of Terra Alpha, notably the city. During working hours, the factories were heavily guarded by the Happiness Patrol, and any slackers or truants were harshly dealt with.

Recently, leaders had emerged from the ranks of the drones – leaders committed to revolution and freedom from such a miserable life. One of the most charismatic of these was the poet Edward Z, who had organized secret meetings and spoken out against conditions imposed on the drones. At a recent packed meeting he argued persuasively for civil rights for the drones, who, after all, were producing the planet's wealth. Secret agents from the Happiness Patrol had been present at the meeting; a few days later Edward Z disappeared.

More meetings were arranged, and now the drones had left the factories behind and had marched on the city. Their demonstrations now wound through the streets. Clothed in black suits and bowler hats, and wearing veils to protect their identities, they carried banners proclaiming their message. 'Factory conditions are a joke!' read one. 'Where is Edward Z?' asked another.

Ace was being escorted back to the waiting zone by Daisy K and one of her guards, when she heard the slow drumbeat to which the drones marched. Rounding the next corner, she saw the bizarre procession.

'Evil!' she shouted happily. 'What's going on here?'

Daisy K was trying to ignore the passing drones. 'It's of no consequence,' she said.

They were not the only ones watching the demonstration. Peeking out of a manhole in the corner of the street, Wences was following events with interest. Wences was of the genus Alpidae, which had once lived off the wild sugar-beet. He had his species' characteristically large, pointed ears, and the wrinkled skin which made even the youngest Alpida appear to be ancient. He wore a loose silk robe and held a sharp spear in his paw.

Since the arrival of human life on Terra Alpha, the Alpidae had been forced underground, and they now lived off the sugar deposited in the large pipes which connected the sugar factories all over the planet to the city. It was for this reason that Helen A, who often hunted the Alpidae with Fifi, called them Pipe People.

Ace, who had not seen Wences, read the banners carried by the drones and watched the shuffling gait of the demonstrators. 'I'd say they were rather upset about something,' she said.

Daisy K could not hide her fury. 'They're fools,' she snapped. 'They think they can achieve something with their march.'

Ace could see that they had already managed to infuriate

55

Daisy K. She was on their side for that alone. 'A demonstration!' she cried. 'Wicked!'

Wences, in his manhole, was delighted.

Daisy K's voice hardened. 'All they will achieve is their extinction.'

Ace wasn't surprised. 'So Helen A doesn't allow demos. I could have guessed as much.'

Daisy K looked horrified at the suggestion. 'Of course she allows demonstrations. But these are killjoys – and worse than that, they're drones.'

Ace hadn't heard of them. 'Drones?'

Daisy K explained. 'Workers from the flatlands. It is forbidden for them to visit the city.' She smiled grimly. 'That's why they won't leave it alive.'

Then Ace understood. 'You're scared of them, aren't you?'

Daisy K avoided the question. 'They will be dealt with in good time,' she said.

Ace struggled free and shouted with all her might. 'Up the killjoys! The drones united will never be defeated!'

Daisy K cuffed her sharply on the back of the head. 'Silence!'

'Gordon Bennett!' shouted Ace, just before a handkerchief was stuffed into her mouth. She was marched quickly away from the demonstration.

Wences had watched all of this scene from his manhole. He took one last look at the drones and was gone, hidden once more in the underground city of the sugar pipes.

The Kandy Man had finished with Earl, at least for the time being. Earl was slumped in his chair, unconscious, but with a beatific smile stretching from ear to ear.

'He looks as if he enjoyed it,' noted the Doctor.

The Kandy Man looked up from his work. 'I'd be very angry if he hadn't.'

The Doctor listened to the whistle of Earl's soft snore. 'But he's still very much alive.'

'The night is young,' said the Kandy Man, ominously.

56

He examined a line of bottles. 'Now, let's see what we've got for you.'

'Just before we start,' said the Doctor, 'I wonder if I could ask you about something which has been worrying me. It's the executions.'

The Kandy Man continued his selection of the coloured liquids. 'What about them?'

The Doctor continued. 'It's just that out there nobody seems to know what method you use. I was intrigued.'

The Doctor had clearly touched on a subject that was dear to the Kandy Man's heart. He placed a bottle on the table and moved over to the Doctor's chair. 'I didn't realize that you were concealing an interest in the mechanics of execution, Doctor. A man after my own soft-centre.'

The Doctor tried to shrug. 'Just curious.'

'Do you think we should grant him a last wish, Gilbert?'

Gilbert was checking lists of required ingredients. 'Whatever you think, Kandy Man.' He hurried out of the kitchen with his lists.

'I don't see why not.' After his success with Earl, the Kandy Man was in a good mood. He stomped over to one of the great silver pipes leading from one side of the kitchen to the other and slapped it with his sticky hand. It made a hollow, booming sound. 'The secret's in the pipes. Vanilla secret, tomorrow, I think.' He allowed himself a moment to chuckle at his little joke. 'Just when the victim thinks he's been pardoned it flows into the yard and smothers him. Ingenious, isn't it?'

'It's depraved!'

'We call it the fondant surprise!'

'Can it be stopped once it's in motion?'

'The foam can be diverted down another pipe.' Suddenly the Kandy Man was cautious again. 'But I'm not going to tell you how. Anyway, it's a hypothetical question. What reason could I possibly have for stopping an execution?'

The Doctor had noticed a large bottle marked 'lemonade' behind the Kandy Man's right shoulder. He changed the subject. 'Just now, you said soft-centre.'

57

'Did I?'

'You said soft-centre instead of heart. Exactly what is your heart made of?'

The Kandy Man liked this question. He liked talking about himself. 'Difficult to say. It's all in there somewhere. Caramel, sherbet, toffee, marzipan, gelling agents. But it's all in motion.'

'A movable feast, eh?' said the Doctor.

'Very droll, Doctor.'

But the Doctor now had the knowledge that he needed. He had a plan. 'So you're perfectly adapted to your environment,' he said.

'Perfectly,' the Kandy Man smiled.

The Doctor knew that the Kandy Man's constitution would not be able to bear intense heat. He had noted with regret that all the ovens in the kitchen were tightly secured. Still, the Kandy Man had his back to the bank of ovens, so he wouldn't know that.

He spoke to the Kandy Man. 'You're protected against everything, in fact, except the intense heat of the open stove behind you.'

'What?'

'I said protected against everything except the intense heat of the open stove behind . . .'

'Silence!' bellowed the Kandy Man as he spun round to see if the stove was open. But, as the Doctor had planned, he spun round too quickly, and his shoulder crashed into the shelf of bottles, causing the large bottle of lemonade to crash to the floor. For the Doctor had also realized that there was something else that would render the Kandy Man defenceless.

'And, of course, the adhesive qualities of carbonated aitch-two-O and citric acid.'

The lemonade had spilt over the Kandy Man's feet. He was thrashing about trying to move. But he was stuck! – stuck to the floor by a bottle of lemonade. The humiliation! He cried out for Gilbert M, but to no avail. He still hadn't returned from his errand. The Kandy Man was helpless.

The Doctor had taken special notice of the knots that Gilbert M had used when tying him up. They weren't very complicated – the Doctor had taught the youthful Houdini how to wriggle free of them – and he proceeded to do that himself.

In the next chair, Earl groaned. He was coming round.

'Lemonade, to you,' said the Doctor, untying him. He slapped Earl's face. 'Come on, the dream's over. Back to the nightmare.'

He pushed Earl down through the open manhole and jumped down after him. Moments later he reappeared to recover Earl's harmonica, which had been left lying on the floor. The Kandy Man was still making vain attempts to free his feet and shouting for Gilbert M. The Doctor doffed his hat. 'Sweet dreams,' he said.

The Kandy Man's strength had all but ebbed when Gilbert M returned to the Kandy Kitchen, ambling in with a large sack. Summoning all his remaining energy, the Kandy Man screamed at him. 'Where have you been?'

Gilbert M dumped the sack on the floor. 'Ingredients,' he said, unconcerned.

'Leaving me to be humiliated. You'll suffer for this.'

Gilbert M stifled a yawn. 'Whatever you say, Kandy Man.'

'You'll pay for this,' the Kandy Man threatened. 'I'm going to crush you.'

Gilbert M moved over to the part of the kitchen where the Kandy Man was stuck, but made no attempt to help him. 'That's it,' he said, 'scream and shout; rant and rave – but remember, Kandy Man, symbiosis.' The Kandy Man snarled, but Gilbert M continued. 'You need me and I need me.'

'You need you?'

'I need me.'

'I need you and you need you?'

Gilbert M was triumphant. 'That's what I said. And just as you squeeze the breath out of me so your hand tightens round your own throat!'

* * *

The Doctor and Earl were slowly making their way along one of the huge pipes running beneath the city. It was cold and dank, and their passage was marked by the drip, drip, drip of liquid from the roof and the walls. The Doctor touched one of the walls and licked his finger.

'It's a sort of crystallized sugar,' he told Earl, 'almost like a meringue. The walls are covered with it. I suppose the pipe must have carried some sort of sugar solution. What do you think?'

Earl tasted the substance. He shook his head. 'No good. But then I've tasted the real thing.'

The Doctor tried some more, from a different part of the wall. 'It's definitely past its best, so we can assume that nothing's been pumped down here for quite a while. I wonder why.' He turned to Earl. He was curious about something. 'So how would you describe the Kandy Man's confection?' he asked.

Earl smiled. 'It could only be the work of a schizophrenic obsessive.' Earl took his harmonica from his jacket pocket. But the Doctor stopped him just as he was about to start playing.

He pointed to the ceiling. 'Not until we're out of this section,' whispered the Doctor.

'Why are we whispering?' whispered Earl.

'There are tons of crystallized syrup above us.'

Earl understood. 'And any sudden noise could cause it to fall.'

'Not any noise,' said the Doctor, 'only certain noises.'

'That's reassuring,' said Earl, slipping the harmonica back into his pocket. They moved on down the tunnel, completely unaware of the small figures following them and watching their every move.

A few hundred yards further along, the Doctor held up his hand to stop Earl. He suddenly dropped to the ground to examine something that had caught his attention. 'Look at this, Earl,' he whispered. 'It's some kind of print.'

Earl could just make it out. But for all his interplanetary

travelling he had never seen anything quite like it before. 'I wonder what sort of creature lives down here?'

Before he finished speaking, one of the Pipe People, brandishing his spear, moved out of the shadows.

'That sort of creature,' said the Doctor.

Earl and the Doctor were taken to an intersection of pipes, where there was evidence of habitation, a pile of straw in one corner, and some basic eating utensils stacked in another. They were guarded by one of the Pipe People. He was nervy and ignored all of the Doctor's many attempts at an explanation. So they were relieved to see the approach of Wences, who had watched Ace at the demonstration. He was with Wulfric, who seemed older and more experienced than the others. The Doctor correctly assumed that Wulfric was the leader of this tribe.

'Stand!' ordered Wulfric. The Pipe People did not speak the settlers' tongue, but had picked up a smattering of the language of their enemies, in the same way that countries at war begin to learn the language of their opponents. But their grasp of syntax was shaky and they generally confined themselves to monosyllabic utterances.

The Doctor and Earl pulled themselves to their feet.

'Weapons!' barked Wulfric. His voice was high-pitched but clear.

The Doctor held his hands above his head and twirled round for Wulfric's benefit. 'No weapons,' he said. 'Just a brolly.'

Wulfric turned to Earl. 'Weapons!'

Earl copied the Doctor. But as he spun round, his harmonica flew out of his pocket and fell to the floor.

Wences raised his spear, ready to attack. 'Weapon!' he shrieked.

Earl bent down slowly and picked up the harmonica. 'Easy,' he said, 'it's just my harp.' He put it to his lips to demonstrate. As he did so, everyone except the Doctor ducked, obviously expecting a missile to fly out of it. But all that came out of it were a few slow, sad notes. It was clear that the Pipe People responded to the music immediately.

'Wicked!' squealed Wences.

The Doctor could not believe his ears. 'What did you just say?'

'Wicked!'

Earl was impressed. 'Say, Doctor, he's hip for a little guy!'

But the Doctor was one step ahead of Earl. 'He's been taking lessons,' he said. He bent down to Wences. 'So you've met my friend Ace?'

'Not Ace,' said Wences.

'Brave girl,' said Wulfric, who had heard Wences's account of Ace's defiance of the Happiness Patrol.

'Captive,' said Wences.

The Doctor shook his head. 'Brave girl captive. That sounds like Ace. If only she'd listen to what I tell her.'

'Not Ace,' Wulfric insisted.

'Gordon,' said Wences.

'Gordon?' asked Earl.

'Gordon?' asked the Doctor.

'Bennett!' squealed Wences.

The Happiness Patrol guards had departed and had left Ace in the waiting zone, staring at her old adversary Priscilla P. But this wasn't the same waiting zone. It was similar, in that again it was lit by a single streetlight, and again it was taped off from the rest of the street, but Ace didn't recognize the surrounding buildings. Then she understood that the waiting zone moved round the city according to the whim of Helen A.

'Wotcher!' she said to Priscilla P, trying to get a reaction. 'I like your new prison.'

Priscilla P advanced on her. 'On Terra Alpha . . .'

The old spiel, about to be reeled off parrot-like. Ace interrupted her. 'Yeah, yeah, I know. On Terra Alpha you don't have prisons.'

But Priscilla P wouldn't be stopped. 'We have the waiting

zone instead. And the waiting zone moves to different places in the city according to the time of the night.'

Ace had heard enough. 'Waiting zone! Who do you think you're kidding?'

Priscilla P took out her gun, inspected it, and then blew down the barrel. She looked over at Ace and smiled. 'Some people don't have to remain in the waiting zone very long.'

Ace, showing great restraint, decided it would be politic to keep quiet, at least for a few minutes. Priscilla P put the gun back and rummaged in her tray. She pulled out one of the cans of nitro-nine confiscated from Ace during her first brief stay in the waiting zone. She showed it to Ace. 'What's this?'

Ace moved towards her. 'I'll show you . . .' But Priscilla P had produced her gun again. Ace backed off. 'Just trying to be friendly,' she said innocently.

Priscilla P returned to the nitro-nine. 'It's an explosive device of some kind. I used to work with explosives when I was in Happiness Patrol B.' She sounded almost wistful. 'The anti-terrorist squad. We worked the night shift – I like working at night.'

'I'm not interested,' said Ace.

But Priscilla P did not hear. 'And anyway, night-time is when they come out.'

Ace, despite herself, was curious. 'Who?'

'Killjoys – depressives. Manic, reactive, endogenous – we got all of them.'

'What do you mean, got them?'

Priscilla turned to Ace, delighted that she had at last got an audience. 'They disappeared.'

Ace had been in Terra Alpha long enough to know what this euphemism meant. 'You make me sick,' she snarled.

But Priscilla P only smiled. 'I did a good job.'

Ace had heard this before. 'Yeah, right, you were only doing your job.'

'And then they put me on this. It was unfair. I knew the streets – I was a fighter.'

63

'No you weren't,' said Ace, not bothering to try to conceal the contempt in her voice. 'You were a killer.'

'And she still is.' It was a new voice, and Ace turned to see Susan Q being escorted into the waiting zone by two Happiness Patrol guards.

When the guards had left, Priscilla P regarded Susan Q with hostility. 'I am what I am,' she said.

Ace felt guilty about Susan Q. When she had taken the key from her at the Happiness Patrol headquarters she hadn't considered the consequences for Susan Q. Later, when they were sitting against a wall and out of earshot of Priscilla P, she apologized.

'It's all my fault,' said Ace. 'You'd be all right if you hadn't met me.'

But Susan Q shook her head. 'It would have happened sooner or later. I'm not Helen A's idea of good Happiness Patrol material. She won't shed any tears over me. Let's face it, no one will.' She smiled. 'Even if they wanted to it wouldn't be allowed.'

'But what now?' Ace was worried.

'I'll just disappear along with the rest of them,' shrugged Susan Q. 'Just another of Helen A's victims.'

'I won't let it happen.' said Ace, gritting her teeth. 'We'll escape. I'll save you.'

Susan Q laughed softly. 'Don't worry. I'm happy that it's finally over. It's funny that, isn't it? It's the first thing that I've been happy about for ages.'

Even as they spoke, Helen A was planning the demise of Susan Q. She was in the headquarters of the Happiness Patrol, sitting at a console with Daisy K at her side. Helen A flicked a switch and spoke into a microphone. 'Happiness will prevail. Happiness Patrol C please assume positions for the first stage of a routine disappearance. And don't forget, when you smile I want to see those teeth.' She switched off the microphone and smiled sweetly at Daisy K. 'I think I'll let you handle this one, Daisy,' she said. 'Susan Q was a friend of yours, wasn't she?'

Moments later, the Happiness Patrol guards arrived at the waiting zone and hauled Susan Q to her feet.

'Time for you to go,' said Priscilla P.

Susan Q struggled with the guards but they were too strong for her.

Ace leapt up, ready to take on the guards. 'Leave her alone!'

'I'm not ready!' cried Susan Q.

'No one ever is,' said Priscilla P, quietly, and levelled her gun at Ace, who was moving towards Susan Q. 'Steady,' she said.

Susan was still struggling in vain. 'Wait a minute! Just let me say goodbye to my friend. Please!'

Priscilla P walked up to Susan Q and looked into her eyes. 'Why?' she said softly. 'What's the point?' Then she turned to the guards and her voice hardened. 'Take her away!'

As the guards dragged Susan Q away to the nearby Happiness Patrol jeep, Ace glared at Priscilla P. 'Just one question. How do you live with yourself?'

Priscilla P watched as the jeep drove off down the road. Susan Q had been in her patrol on the night shift. Priscilla P thought she had an attitude problem, always trying to understand the killjoys they found, instead of eliminating them. Always wanting an hour-long debate before using her fun gun. As far as Priscilla P was concerned, Susan Q was the sort of guard the Happiness Patrol could do without. She felt no remorse as she watched Susan Q being taken to her death.

She said as much to Ace. 'She was never any good. She never had the right attitude. She never joined in. She wasn't part of the team. She . . .'

Ace clamped her hands over her ears. 'She was my friend!'

Suddenly Priscilla P was diving to the ground, pulling her gun. Ace instinctively leapt for cover, but then saw that Priscilla P was not aiming at her, but at a small creature emerging from a manhole just down the street. It was Wences, who had been sent out to look for Ace.

Priscilla fired, but Wences ducked down into the pipe and safety. When he emerged again he threw his small spear with all his strength. Priscilla P dodged it, but lost her balance. Ace took her chance and lunged at Priscilla P, slamming her to the ground, and knocking her gun out of her hand. The tray was upset, and Ace managed to rescue one of her cans of nitro-nine.

'Ace!' It was Wences, calling from the manhole.

Ace hesitated, and then ran for the manhole. She jumped into it, following Wences, just as Priscilla P recovered her gun and opened fire.

8

In another section of the pipes, the Pipe People were guiding Earl and the Doctor to a manhole leading to the surface. Wulfric was leading the way. He had already fallen once on the journey. Now he lost his footing and collapsed again.

Earl helped him up. 'What's the matter with these little guys?'

The Doctor was concerned. 'They may not look like it,' he said, 'but they're on the edge of starvation.' He tapped the wall with his umbrella. 'No sugar in the pipes.'

'But why can't they live on the surface?'

They used to,' said the Doctor, grimly. 'They were driven down here by the human settlers.'

'Can't someone help them?'

'Yes,' said the Doctor. 'Us.'

They stopped and Wulfric pointed to the roof. 'Here we are,' said the Doctor. 'Seventh manhole on the left. I'll go first.' He turned to face Wulfric and doffed his hat. 'Thank you, Wulfric. It has been my privilege.'

The Doctor scrambled up the side of the pipe and pushed open the manhole. He hooked his umbrella to the side of the hole and pulled himself up. As he emerged into the murky gloom of the street, he found himself looking straight at the familiar bowler hat, clipboard and yellow tie of Trevor Sigma.

'Name?' said Trevor Sigma.

'I'm the Doctor. Haven't we met before?'

'I'm sorry,' said Trevor. 'That's classified information.'

'You're Trevor Sigma, aren't you?'

Trevor flipped open his identity card. 'Galactic Census Bureau. I ask the questions.'

'You ask the questions?'

'I'm sorry – that's classified information. Address?'

'Which one?' asked the Doctor.

Trevor Sigma took a deep breath. 'If you live here I need a town and a street. If you're an alien I need a home planet except when you spend more than half of the working year away, in which case I need a planet of origin.'

'I'm sorry that's classified information. Name?'

Trevor Sigma was nonplussed. 'What?'

'I ask the questions,' snapped the Doctor. 'Name?'

'Trevor Sigma.'

'Address?'

'Galactic Centre.'

Earl pulled himself up through the manhole. 'What's going on?'

'Questionnaire,' said the Doctor.

'I hate questionnaires,' groaned Earl.

The Doctor turned his attention back to Trevor Sigma. 'Occupation?'

'Galactic census taker,' said Trevor, obediently. 'Authorized to enter any Alphan property and interview all Alphans.'

This was what the Doctor had been waiting to hear. 'I thought so. Good,' he said. 'Take me to their leader.'

Earl had his own plans. 'I've got places to go, Doctor,' he said.

'Don't worry,' said the Doctor. 'I'll find you when I need you.'

'How?'

'The brandy of the damned, of course.'

Earl slapped the Doctor on the back. 'Listen, Doctor. You're a nice guy but a little weird.'

'Music, Earl,' explained the Doctor. 'Play the blues for me.'

Earl waved, and ambled off down the street. As he went

68

he took his harmonica out of his jacket pocket and started to play.

Trevor Sigma and the Doctor watched him go, and listened to the haunting music.

'That's nice,' said Trevor, quietly. 'Makes me feel sort of . . .' He struggled for the words.

The Doctor helped him out. 'Melancholy.'

'Yes,' said Trevor, seizing on the word. 'That's it! A pleasant melancholy.'

Daisy K was feeling uncomfortable. She had once again been summoned to see Helen A to account for the events which had taken place at the waiting zone. Helen A sat before her, stroking Fifi, who purred contentedly. Suddenly Helen A fixed Daisy K in her gaze and spoke.

'I still don't understand,' she said, 'how Priscilla P, one of our most enthusiastic happiness crusaders . . .'

Daisy K snorted. Priscilla P had got her into enough trouble recently for her to have any vestige of sympathy.

Helen A pretended not to hear, and continued '. . . how Priscilla P came to be overpowered by a defenceless girl.'

'The girl wasn't alone,' said Daisy K.

'Then tell me about her companions,' smiled Helen A. 'We need that sort of spirit in the Happiness Patrol.'

Daisy K wished she had kept her mouth shut. 'The girl was in league with a vermin,' she said, realizing how ridiculous it sounded even as she was saying it.

Helen A was beginning to enjoy herself. 'So Priscilla P was defeated by a defenceless girl and a vermin. Is it a joke, Daisy K?'

Daisy K bowed her head. 'No, ma'am.'

Helen A sat back in her chair. 'What a shame. I enjoy a good joke. Tell me. Where did this guerrilla unit disappear to when it had dealt with Priscilla P?'

'It went down the pipes,' said Daisy K, praying for the end of this inquisition.

But Helen A seemed pleased. 'The pipes. Excellent,' she said, stroking Fifi, who growled softly. 'Fifi's been eating too many chocolates recently, haven't you my darling?' She planted a kiss on the top of Fifi's head. Then her voice hardened. 'She could do with a bit of sport!'

Under the ground, Ace was padding along one of the larger pipes. The bottom of the pipe was sticky and the going was difficult. Every now and then she had to wait for Wences, whose legs were much shorter than hers, to catch up. He arrived at her side, and rested for a moment, leaning against the side of the pipe.

'Nice pipes,' said Ace, making conversation. 'Reminds me of Perivale.'

'Ace!' said Wences.

'Well, not that nice!' said Ace, puzzled by his reaction.

'Gordon Bennett!' said Wences. He shifted the position of the can of nitro-nine, which, as a warrior, he had insisted on carrying.

'And careful with that can, or we'll end up as graffiti,' said Ace. They had rested long enough now, and continued trudging along the pipe.

Up ahead, a manhole slid open and Happiness Patrol hands gently lowered a small bedraggled bundle into the pipe. Fifi threw back her head and howled with pleasure. She was hunting again.

Earl was sitting on a white wrought-iron chair on the balcony of a deserted house, his feet resting on the rail. He was in no hurry, just enjoying the sounds of his harmonica in the night air. He had never known a city that was so silent. He knew the Happiness Patrol curfew was in operation, but even so there were no sounds from the surrounding houses and no sounds of life, not even a passing space-shuttle in the sky.

Suddenly there was a new sound. Earl stopped playing and listened. It was a slow, rhythmic drumbeat, and a solemn chant. The sound was getting closer and from his vantage-point he had a clear view of the drones' procession as it shuffled round the corner into the street below. He watched for a few moments, and then went back into the empty house and slipped out of a back door. The Doctor should know about this.

From a higher balcony a few streets away, a couple of trained killers were waiting for the procession to come past. David S and Alex S were Happiness Patrol snipers. In spite of their lowly names, they had done well to get as far as they had done in a woman's world. There were few men in the Happiness Patrol – only a small squad of unarmed Happiness Patrol men of immense physical strength, and another of trained marksmen, of which David S and Alex S were a part. But even these groups were discriminated against. Picking off drones taking part in a hopeless demonstration against Happiness Patrol murders was not high-profile work.

They huddled together against the cold while they were waiting, listening to the approaching drumbeat. Eventually, David S decided they should prepare. He carefully unwrapped his pride and joy – a new gun.

'Here we are,' he said. 'Look at that.'

But Alex S was too miserable to be interested. 'I can't believe we're doing this again.'

David S stroked the gun affectionately. 'The mark three.'

Alex S shook his head. 'Roof duty!'

'The prototype for the mark four must be ready,' said David S, peering through the telescopic sight. 'For the women, of course,' he added glumly.

'You don't see any women doing roof duty, do you?' moaned Alex S. 'Women always get the better jobs.'

'Women always get the best guns.'

But Alex was preoccupied. He had recently made the biggest mistake you could make in his job – he had started thinking about it. He had looked at what he was doing with his life and hadn't liked what he'd seen. But he hadn't spoken to anyone about it, and it took courage to mention it to David S.

'It's supposed to be an easy job,' he said. 'Just look through the sights and make up your mind. Are they

71

behaving properly? Are they happy? If not, pull the trigger.' It was ironic, he felt, because he certainly wouldn't regard himself as a happy man.

But David S was still admiring his gun. 'Still, I'm not complaining. Less jamming on the mark three.'

'The problem is, it gets too easy to pull the trigger,' said Alex S.

'Smoother trigger action on the mark three.'

'Are you listening to what I'm saying?' Alex S exploded. 'Don't you see what we're doing?'

David S took another long look through the sights. 'High-power sights.'

'I'm talking to you!'

David S turned slowly, raising his gun so that its barrel rested on Alex S's throat. 'It's a gun for the job,' he said.

9

Trevor Sigma led the Doctor to the residence of Helen A and Joseph C. In common with most Alphan buildings, from the outside it looked as if it had seen better days. The Doctor could see that once it would have been most imposing, as it was a large building set back from the street. But now the garden wall was crumbling and the whole edifice needed a coat of paint. A couple of the attic windows were broken.

The only thing that now set it apart from other buildings in this part of the city were the Happiness Patrol guards at ease beside the rusty gates. The Doctor's way in was temporarily barred by the guards, but Trevor Sigma's identification worked like a magic key, and soon they were striding across the neglected rosebeds to the front door. Helen A's spies had obviously given her advance warning of Trevor Sigma's visit, and she had given orders to let him pass. The Doctor noted that, for the time being at least, she was trying to present an untroubled face to the Galactic Bureau.

Joseph C answered the door and showed them through to Helen A's suite. The Doctor saw Helen A before she saw him. What he saw was a woman of immense presence, beautifully groomed, wearing her deep crimson velvet suit proudly, as if it was some kind of exotic plumage. Her blonde and mauve hair was perfectly sculpted and topped by a matching crimson feather hat. When the Doctor walked into the room, she was curled up on the sofa with a book of photographs, laughing to herself as she turned the pages. As soon as she heard their entrance she quickly hid the book behind the cushions. It was a luxurious apartment, with a black and white colour scheme and stylish, comfortable furniture. Helen A's world might be crashing around her ears, thought the Doctor, but she isn't making any sacrifices.

Joseph C motioned them in. 'It's Trevor Sigma, dear,' he said, 'and, er . . .' He waved vaguely at the Doctor.

Helen A leapt up from the sofa. 'Trevor Sigma! Delighted to see you again,' she smiled and turned to the Doctor. 'I don't think we've had the pleasure.'

'It's no pleasure, I assure you,' he said lightly.

'How kind,' beamed Helen A, but the Doctor had seen the momentary clouding of her eyes which indicated that she had heard exactly what he had said.

But Joseph C seemed pleased to see him. 'Are you with the bureau as well?' he enquired politely.

The Doctor was civil. 'I'm sorry, that's classified information.' He spun round to face Helen A. 'I understand you're responsible for this planet.'

'We do our best.'

'And is it a happy planet?'

Helen A disliked being interrogated. 'I think you'll find everyone on Terra Alpha is very happy,' she said firmly.

But the Doctor would not be placated. 'Some people on Terra Alpha are very hard to find,' he said.

Helen A gritted her teeth, and then smiled charmingly. 'Then I'm sure Trevor will sniff them out for you, won't you Trevor?'

'I'm sorry,' said the Doctor, cutting in, 'he can't answer that.'

Helen A ignored him and turned her attention to Trevor, now ensconced in a deep easy chair. 'I'm glad you're here, Trevor. I wanted to tell you that I've adopted the bureau's recommendations on population control.'

This interested the Doctor. 'Which were?' he asked.

'To control it,' said Helen A simply.

Trevor Sigma shook his head. 'Not my department.'

74

But Helen A would not be put off her success story. 'We've controlled the population down by seventeen per cent.'

'I'm sure you have,' said the Doctor.

Helen A smiled at him. 'Overcrowding has been quite eliminated,' she said.

'No more queues at the post office,' put in Joseph C, helpfully.

The Doctor ignored him. 'And you used the bureau's programme?' he asked Helen A.

'Not quite,' she said. 'I found that my own programme was more effective.' She was interrupted by the sharp monotone of a bleeper. She reached into a pocket and the sound stopped. 'Do excuse me, gentlemen,' she said sweetly, her eyes embracing her guests. 'Joseph C will look after you.' Helen A swept out of the room.

Joseph C's reaction to his wife's unexpected departure was usually a smart move towards the drinks cabinet, and this time was no exception. Helen A had banned alcohol from the palace several months before but the feel of a glass in his hand still gave Joseph a sense of security.

When Trevor joined Joseph at the sideboard the Doctor decided to take the weight off his feet and jumped on to Helen A's sofa. But he couldn't get comfortable. There was something under the cushion. The Doctor fished around, making sure that Joseph's attentions were elsewhere, and finally produced Helen A's photograph album, which had been under the cushions. He turned the pages. Shots of Helen A in a garden with a ball, Helen A on a picnic in the country, Helen A on this very sofa watching television. But the most striking thing about all the photographs was Helen A's companion. The Doctor recognized it immediately as a small female Stigorax. The Doctor did a quick calculation and was surprised at the result. According to him, Stigoraxes should be extinct in Terra Alpha by now. Something else puzzled him about the photographs. He knew the Stigorax to be one of the most ferocious and ruthless predators in the universe, and yet in these pictures the animal looked happy and relaxed, like some idiot domestic dog from twentieth century Earth.

Joseph C and Trevor Sigma had helped themselves to drinks and had finished at the sideboard, so the Doctor quickly hid the photograph album behind the cushion again.

Joseph was complaining loudly about the frequency of Trevor Sigma's visits. 'I say, Trevor, do we have to go through with this census business again? Things haven't changed much since you were last here.'

The Doctor found this hard to believe. 'Haven't they?' he said.

But Trevor knew his orders. 'Full planetary census every six local cycles. It's the rules.'

'But couldn't you . . . ?'

The Doctor interrupted Joseph C. 'No, he couldn't.'

Joseph C resigned himself to the inconvenience. 'Very well. A quick lemonade and then I'll show you round the floral clock. How about, er . . .' He nodded vaguely in the Doctor's direction. 'Is he coming?'

'He can't, I'm afraid,' said the Doctor. 'He has a prior engagement.' The Doctor leapt up from the sofa and headed for the door through which Helen A had made her exit.

Trevor Sigma called after him. 'Where are you going?'

The Doctor turned back. 'Remember, Trevor,' he said, 'I ask the questions.' And with that he slipped out of the room leaving Joseph and Trevor to their speculations.

It didn't take the Doctor long to find the headquarters of the Happiness Patrol, where Helen A sat at the console before a bank of monitors. He crept in unnoticed and leaned against the wall, watching her at work.

Several of the monitors were displaying pictures of the execution yard. It was empty, but decorated with bunting and balloons. The Doctor remembered his visit to the yard, and knew that these decorations signified an imminent execution. Helen A watched the monitors and spoke into a microphone. 'Routine disappearance number five hundred thousand and five,' she announced. 'Calling Happiness

Patrol section C. The preparations are now complete. Stand by to escort killjoy to execution yard.' She signed off: 'Happiness will prevail!'

'Population control?' asked the Doctor quietly.

Helen A spun round in her chair. 'Look,' she said angrily. 'Who are you?'

The Doctor shook his head. 'I'm sorry. I'm not at liberty to say.' He pointed to the monitor. 'And which member of the population are you controlling today? Just for the record.'

'A woman who disappointed me,' sneered Helen A.

'And how did she disappoint you?' asked the Doctor, but stopped her before she could reply. 'No, let me guess. She enjoyed the feel of rain on her face. Or perhaps her favourite season was the autumn.'

Helen A spun round again to face the monitors. 'You talk too much,' she said, 'whoever you are.' She reached under the desk to press a hidden button.

'Is that a question?' said the Doctor.

'No.'

'Good. I'm the Doctor,' he said doffing his hat and leaving. Helen A jabbed furiously at the alarm button under the console. The Doctor popped back into the room. 'Still no joy?' he smiled. 'I should get that button seen to.' And he left again, this time removing a small fire extinguisher from a bracket on the wall as he went. As he went through the doorway, the alarm burst into life and the first Happiness Patrol guard slid down the silver pole into the room, followed by another, and another.

'Find the killjoy,' shouted Helen A as the guards rushed past her and after the Doctor, 'and put him out of his misery. Seal the palace! No more visitors! I don't want this unhappy incident repeated.'

Joseph C was back at the sideboard, organizing a top-up for Trevor Sigma. He was offering him a soda siphon. 'A touch more lemonade?'

The Doctor burst into the room and rushed past, grabbed the siphon as he went by, and jammed it into the jacket pocket not containing the fire extinguisher. 'Thank you, Joseph,' he shouted as he rushed out into the garden heading towards the street.

Joseph C looked quizzically at Trevor Sigma. 'Strange chap,' he said, as the room filled with the Happiness Patrol guards in pursuit of the Doctor.

Ace and Wences were still trudging along the pipe twenty feet under the ground. Wences seemed to be tiring and Ace was beginning to regret agreeing to him carrying the can of nitro-nine. She didn't like to imagine what would happen to them if Wences fell. She was snapped out of her brooding by a low, soft growl. She put out a hand to stop Wences. 'What was that?' she whispered. They stood by the wall of the pipe, peering into the dark.

Wences saw a quick movement in the shadows further up the pipe. 'There!' he said, pointing. But Ace could see nothing. 'Where?' Wences pointed again but the movement had stopped. Ace knew that they should stay still and quiet, that a sudden movement would be disastrous. But she could see that Wences was terrified. She held his arm softly, to try to calm him, but it was too late. He wriggled free and set off down the pipe.

'Run!' he shouted. There was nothing else she could do. Ace ran after him down the pipe, praying that he was keeping a tight hold on the nitro-nine. As they ran, the soft growling grew louder and louder. Whatever the creature was, it was closing on them.

Ace could see that Wences had stopped up in front of her. When she reached him she saw why. They appeared to have reached a dead end. But Wences knew the pipes – surely he wouldn't have lead them into danger. 'Which way?' she shouted desperately.

'Trapped!' Wences had lost his way in his panic.

Ace wedged her back against the wall. Look on the bright side, she thought, at least we can't be attacked from behind. Peering into the darkness she could see a pair of eyes watching them; the growling was louder than before.

The growling became a roar, and suddenly the creature leapt at them. It was so close that Ace could feel its breath on her cheek. 'Gorden Bennett!' she screamed.

But the creature was just toying with them. It fell back, just when she was at its mercy. Now Ace could see it, in the small clearing in front of them, eyeing them up. It was Fifi, pacing backwards and forwards in front of them. Like the lions in London Zoo, thought Ace, only this time it was she and Wences who were captive.

Ace remembered her last meeting with Fifi. She glanced at Wences, cowering at the foot of the wall. 'I don't think she's being friendly this time, either,' said Ace.

Fifi was moving inexorably closer to them, judging the right moment for her kill. Ace was waiting, too, watching Fifi's every move and waiting for her moment. She couldn't afford to make a mistake. Any sudden movement and Fifi would pounce. Ace and Wences moved further back against the wall.

There was a rumbling in the distance – part of the pipe had caved in. Fifi was momentarily distracted by the sound – this was the chance Ace had been waiting for. She turned to Wences. 'The nitro! Give it here!'

Wences was paralysed with fear. 'Eh?'

'The can!'

Wences threw the can to Ace. Fifi saw what was happening and leapt towards them. 'Get down!' yelled Ace. She waited until she could see the small red veins in Fifi's eyes, and threw the can, dropping to the ground.

There was a huge explosion.

10

The Doctor had lost the pursuing Happiness Patrol guards in the alleys and wynds of the city. He was hiding in a small alcove waiting for the search to be called off. When he decided it was safe, he poked his head out. He seemed to be next to a small booth, with the words 'Stage Door' painted roughly above the window. Then the Doctor recognized the steps of the Forum. He was back in the square where the TARDIS had landed earlier in the evening. The Forum Square. He also recognized it as the site of the waiting zone that he had been brought to with Ace, although there was now no sign of the slot machine or Priscilla P. He idly wondered what sort of trouble Ace was getting herself into.

Ernest P, the stage doorman, had done the job all his life. His father had done it, and his father's father before that. Generations of his family had discovered that the best way of dealing with the public was to be rude to them. That way they went away and didn't bother you. Apart from the Happiness Patrol, of course. Ernest P was always pleased to see them.

The Doctor stood at the stage door window and doffed his hat to Ernest P. 'Excuse me, but wasn't this a prison earlier tonight?'

Ernest P did not look up from his paper. 'We don't have prisons on Terra Alpha.'

'Yes, yes, yes,' said the Doctor impatiently. 'A waiting zone, then.'

Ernest P sighed wearily and looked up at the Doctor.

'It's only a waiting zone during certain hours of the night, that is until it's time for the late show at the Forum.'

'The late show?'

'Happiness Patrol auditions.' Ernest P nodded towards the Forum. 'You want the main entrance, mate. Into the Forum Square, up the steps, can't miss it.'

'But I don't want the late show. I'm hiding.'

Ernest P returned to his paper. 'You need a permit to hide here.'

'It's in my other jacket,' said the Doctor.

Ernest had heard it all before. 'And where's that?'

'It's in my *other* jacket,' said the Doctor.

Ernest had heard enough. He slammed down his paper and struggled to his feet. 'Listen, mate. Authorized personnel and late show Happiness Patrol candidates only. That's what the memo said.'

The Doctor thought of Ace again. 'So this is where they test candidates for the Happiness Patrol.'

The sound of boots on stone alerted the Doctor and he ducked back into his hiding place just in time to watch a Happiness Patrol run past, obviously still hunting him. He emerged when they had gone.

Ernest looked after them proudly. 'Some of the successful candidates,' he said.

'Some of the few,' said the Doctor grimly.

Gilbert M was strolling casually round the Kandy Man – who was still stuck to the floor – studying the problem. He came close enough to infuriate the Kandy Man with his freedom, but just far enough away to avoid the Kandy Man's hands as they lashed out in anger.

'What's happening to me?' shouted the Kandy Man. 'Help me!'

Gilbert M remained calm. 'It's quite simple,' he said, relishing the chance to explain the Kandy Man's predicament to him. 'Created out of glucose-based substances as you are, your joints need constant movement to avoid any form of coagulation.'

81

The Kandy Man hated Gilbert M when he adopted this sort of superior attitude. 'What do you mean?' he yelled.

'You're turning into a slab of toffee,' shrugged Gilbert M. He scratched his chin. 'I saw this problem at the planning stage. And then I realized what the solution was,' he added tantalizingly.

The Kandy Man roared. 'And what was that?'

Gilbert M slowly shook his head. 'I've forgotten.'

'You've forgotten!'

'But I made a note.'

The Kandy Man breathed a huge sigh of relief. 'Luckily for you,' he snarled.

'But I lost it,' smiled Gilbert M.

The Doctor slapped his pockets, to check that he still had the fire extinguisher and the soda siphon, and followed the mellow harmonica music until he found Earl busking on a street corner. There was no one around.

'What did you find out?' asked the Doctor.

Earl took the harmonica from his lips. 'There's a demonstration by workers from the sugar factories. They're striking about the murders committed by the Happiness Patrol.'

The Doctor didn't seem surprised. 'I'll come and talk to them,' he said.

'It's too dangerous,' said Earl. 'At the moment they're pinned down by a couple of snipers.'

The Doctor shrugged. 'I might as well,' he said. 'I've got to go that way to get to the Kandy Kitchen.' There was still an execution to stop.

'The Kandy Kitchen!' Earl was shocked. He never wanted to go anywhere near the Kandy Kitchen again.

The Doctor reassured him. 'Don't worry,' he said. 'I'll deal with the snipers first.' He patted Earl on the shoulder and disappeared into the night. Earl put the harmonica back to his lips and started playing again.

Three streets away, the two snipers, David S and Alex S,

were being frustrated by the drones' refusal to offer themselves for target practice. After the first few rounds they
had all disappeared into the shadows. Alex S had already
given up, and was sitting with his feet resting on the
balcony rail. David S, ever hopeful, was scanning the street
through the sights on his gun. He disliked Alex's attitude
and pushed his feet off the rail. 'Pick up your gun,' he said.

'Why?' asked Alex, replacing his feet. 'There's no one
there.'

David couldn't argue with this. 'You're right. They've
all gone to ground.'

'I don't mind. Good luck to them.'

David S hated that sort of talk. 'Shut it!' he said sharply.
He looked out over the street and saw a figure coming
towards them through the darkness. 'Wait a minute,' he
said softly. 'There's one.' He watched as the Doctor ran
across the street below towards the iron spiral staircase
leading up to the balcony. David S had him in his sights.
'It's all right. I'll have him. Just let him get a little closer.'
His finger squeezed the trigger.

The gun was suddenly knocked out of his hands. It was
Alex S, who had leapt up and was now confronting David.

'Wait!' said Alex. 'He's not a drone.'

David S was startled. He had never seen Alex like this
before. But he was ready to fight. He disguised his punch,
and Alex took it cleanly on the jaw and fell to the floor of
the balcony. David picked up his rifle and pressed the
muzzle gently against Alex's throat. 'He's fair game,' said
David softly. He moved the muzzle up to Alex's forehead.
'And you're headed that way.'

They were distracted by the noisy rattle of the fire escape
as the Doctor ran up to them. When he reached the top the
first thing he saw was David's gun, levelled at him.

'All right,' sneered David. 'Come and say hallo.'

The Doctor doffed his hat. 'Hallo,' he said as he moved
towards David.

Alex, still on the floor, tried to warn the Doctor. 'Get
back! He'll use the gun.'

'Yes, I imagine he will,' said the Doctor. He turned to face David S. 'You like guns, don't you?' The Doctor advanced on him.

David was enjoying himself. He was interested in the situation from a professional point of view. 'This is a specialized weapon,' he told the Doctor. 'Designed for roof duty – designed for long range. I've never used one close-up before.'

'Let him go,' said Alex, desperately.

'No.'

'No, don't,' smiled the Doctor. 'In fact, let's get a little closer.' And still the Doctor moved towards David.

The first flickers of alarm showed in David's eyes. 'Stay where you are,' he ordered the Doctor.

'Why?' asked the Doctor, as he inched forwards. 'Scared? Why should you be scared? You're the one with the gun.'

'That's right,' said David S breathlessly, reassuring himself.

'And you like guns,' smiled the Doctor.

'He'll kill you,' shouted Alex.

'Of course,' said the Doctor, 'that's what guns are for. Press the trigger and end a life. Simple, isn't it?'

'Yes,' said David S.

'Life killing life.'

But David S wasn't sure any more. 'Yes,' he repeated mechanically.

Alex was beginning to notice the extraordinary effect the Doctor was having on David. 'Who are you?'

'Shut up,' ordered the Doctor. He turned back to David. 'So why don't you do it?' he asked. 'Go ahead. Look me in the eye. Pull the trigger. End my life.'

David S was shaking all over. He raised his gun, pointed it at the Doctor's head, and held it there, as steady as he could, for several long moments. Then he lowered it. 'No,' he said softly.

The Doctor looked disappointed. 'Why not?'

'I can't.'

'But why not?'

'I don't know.'

'You don't, do you,' said the Doctor. He turned to Alex. 'Throw away your gun,' he said. Alex obediently took the gun from his shoulder and threw it over the balcony rail into the street below.

The Doctor held out his hands and David placed his gun in them. Still looking into David's eyes, the Doctor threw the gun after Alex's. Then he hurried away down the metal stairs, leaving the snipers to contemplate their encounter with him. The Doctor consulted his watch. This had taken longer than he thought it would, and there was an execution to stop.

The final arrangements were being made in the execution yard for the death of Susan Q. From her position under the enormous pipe in the centre of the yard, she looked round at what she expected to be her last view of Terra Alpha. The multicoloured balloons, the bunting, the line of Happiness Patrol guns. Daisy K was on the ground beneath her reading interminably from an official document. She sounded as if she was reaching the end of her speech. Susan Q listened to what she had to say.

'And so you are sentenced,' intoned Daisy K, 'to the severest penalty decreed by Helen A.'

Susan Q was defiant. 'I'm glad,' she said clearly, so that everyone in the yard could hear.

Daisy K smiled at her. 'I'm happy you're glad,' she said, and turned to face the Happiness Patrol. 'Patrol dismissed!'

Susan Q was taken aback to see the guards shoulder their guns and march out of the yard.

Ace glanced anxiously back along the pipe. There was no sign of Fifi. She didn't see how anything could have withstood the force of the explosion but she wasn't going to take any chances. She tightened her grip on Wences, and struggled on down the pipe. But Wences was exhausted and she was practically pulling him along. Now he had begun to protest as well. 'No!' he squealed.

Ace was impatient. 'Come on, Wences – hurry!' Again she heard Wences protest. 'What are you moaning about now?'

'Voompip!' shouted Wences, or at least that's what it sounded like to Ace.

'Voompip?' said Ace, puzzled.

This time Wences was more insistent. 'Thompip!'

Ace pulled him along behind her. 'Thompip?'

'Boompip!' shrieked Wences, now highly agitated.

Ace still couldn't hear what he was trying to say. 'Boompip?'

At that moment she lost her footing and started sliding down a long, steep, wide pipe that was slippery underfoot.

'Doompipe!' screamed Wences, now clinging on to Ace in terror. Ace realized that this was what Wences had been trying to say. That the route she had been following was going to lead them straight into the doompipe, the pipe that carried the fondant surprise from the Kandy Kitchen on to the heads of Helen A's victims.

'Doompipe!' shouted Ace, turning to look accusingly at Wences as they slid down, gaining speed and losing control. 'Why didn't you tell me?'

Helen A, in the Happiness Patrol's headquarters, was enjoying watching the scenes from the execution yard on her monitor. She had even taken some pleasure from Susan Q's display of defiance, knowing how futile it was. As she watched, the last Happiness Patrol guard left the yard. Susan Q was left with Daisy K.

'Excellent!' said Helen A softly to herself. 'Time for the fondant surprise.'

She popped a sweet into her mouth and pressed a button on the console in front of her. The button activated the lights in the Kandy Kitchen which indicated to the Kandy Man that it was time to proceed with an execution. Helen A sat back in her chair and waited for the fun to commence.

But Gilbert M and the Kandy Man were otherwise engaged when the light in the skull started flashing. The Kandy Man was still stuck to the floor, and Gilbert M was pacing up and down trying to remember his chemical equations.

'It's something to do with the density of sugar,' he said, scratching his head.

A small loudspeaker in the corner of the kitchen burst into life with a bright trumpet fanfare.

'We seem to have an execution,' said Gilbert M. 'Shall I oblige as you're . . .' he paused and smirked, 'as you're bogged down.'

The Kandy Man lunged out, but Gilbert had skipped nimbly out of his range.

'Just get me unstuck!' bellowed the Kandy Man as Gilbert M turned the small metal wheel to set the fondant surprise in motion. Cogs and wheels started turning slowly and the myriad of pipes running across the walls and ceiling of the kitchen wheezed and clanked into life.

Deep in the doompipe, Ace and Wences paused for a moment when they heard the groanings of the Kandy Kitchen far above them. Ace grabbed Wences and hurried along the pipe.

The viscous liquid was beginning to bubble along the pipes when the Doctor rushed into the Kandy Kitchen, fire extinguisher in one hand and lemonade siphon in the other. The Kandy Man, recognizing his enemy, snarled.

'Don't let the Happiness Patrol catch you looking like that,' said the Doctor cheerily. 'Come on, let's have a smile.'

The Kandy Man took a swipe at the Doctor. 'Unstick me!' he pleaded.

The Doctor's plan was working. It was time for him to put his offer on the table. 'I'll unstick you if you'll divert the flow!' he said.

The Kandy Man ground his teeth, considering his options. After what seemed an eternity to the Doctor, the Kandy Man made his decision. 'It's a deal, he said.

The Doctor warily approached the writhing mass of the

Kandy Man. As soon as he was within range, he squirted water from the fire extinguisher over the Kandy Man's feet. After a brief struggle the Kandy Man stepped free of the pool on the floor. Gilbert M snatched the fire extinguisher from the Doctor and examined it closely. 'Of course!' he said, berating himself. 'I remember now. It's so simple! Water! Now, where are my notes?' He rushed out of the kitchen to commit his new discovery to paper.

The Kandy Man was as good as his word. As soon as he was free he lumbered over to a giant lever, and pulled on it with all of his considerable strength. The Doctor listened with satisfaction as the rushing sounds in the pipes faded away into trickles.

Helen A was angrily drumming her fingers on the front of the console. Her monitor was still tuned in to the picture of the execution yard. Susan Q was still standing under the pipe and Daisy K was still guarding her. But what had happened to the fondant surprise? She had given the signal ages ago and time was passing.

She was wondering what to do next when Joseph C ushered Trevor Sigma into the room. 'It's Trevor, dear,' he whispered into her ear. 'He has a few questions for you.'

'Not now,' snapped Helen A, keeping her eyes on the screen.

Joseph jumped back in surprise. 'I do beg your pardon,' he said. He guided Trevor back to the safety of the doorway, from which they both watched the monitor over Helen's shoulder.

The slope of the pipe was getting steeper and steeper as Ace and Wences scrambled down as fast as they could, away from the rumbling noises behind them. They were both exhausted and wondering how much further they could go. But then, peering into the gloom ahead of them, Ace saw a small pinprick of light. It was the end of the pipe. She took off her rucksack, picked up the ailing Wences and carefully placed him inside. Then she gritted her teeth and marched forward. But suddenly the pipe dipped away from them and they were falling, out of control.

Susan Q and Daisy K were also listening to the sounds coming from the pipe. Susan Q still did not know what to expect. Daisy K, who had supervised many executions before, was beginning to suspect that something had gone badly wrong. The familiar rushing sound which normally built up to the moment of death was fading away, and had been replaced by a clattering sound. She was watching the end of the pipe suspiciously when Ace came flying out, closely followed by Wences.

Ace landed on top of Susan Q and knocked her away from the pipe. 'Get down!' she screamed. As they fell, Wences flew out of the rucksack and into the corner of the yard, where he slipped down a manhole into another, altogether familiar section of the pipe. He was home.

Ace and Susan Q huddled together, to one side of the pipe, and watched the great gaping hole. Daisy K watched from a safe distance. They all listened as the rushing sound stopped and they all watched as one single drop of the fondant surprise lingered on the rim of the pipe, before dripping to the ground. Daisy K sauntered over to Susan and Ace, and jerked her gun at them. 'Get up!' she barked.

Helen A, watching this scene on the monitor in the Happiness Patrol's headquarters, was finding it hard to contain her fury. She had turned a deep red, and small blue veins were throbbing in her neck. She could contain herself no longer.

'They'll suffer for this!' she shouted at the monitor. 'And only when they're screaming to go back under the pipe will I oblige.'

'No,' said a calm reasonable voice behind her. She spun round in her chair. It was Trevor Sigma.

'What?'

'You can't,' he said, adjusting his tie.

Helen A realized with disbelief that Joseph C had let Trevor Sigma watch the whole of the abortive execution on the monitor from behind her.

But Trevor wasn't outraged. He simply wanted to see things done properly. 'Constitutional rules of the system,' he said. 'When the mechanics of an execution malfunction, then the aforementioned execution may not be repeated.'

'I say,' said Joseph, who thought he could see what Trevor was getting at. 'What a nuisance.'

Helen A knew exactly what he was saying. 'So they are now protected from the fondant surprise?'

Trevor Sigma nodded affirmation. 'Rules of the system,' he repeated.

Helen A stood up and advanced menacingly on Trevor Sigma. 'The rules of the system?' she said dangerously.

Trevor Sigma took a pace backwards. He was nervous of Helen A while she was in this mood, and could see a way to help her out of her quandary. 'Which further go on to say that an alternative execution may be substituted.'

Helen A relaxed and smiled. 'Fine,' she said, flashing her eyes at Trevor. 'The Forum.'

The Doctor watched with satisfaction as the last cog stopped turning. He knew he had been in time to stop the execution.

The Kandy Man tightened the last valve and turned to face the Doctor. 'So you trusted me then, Doctor?'

'But of course.'

'Very wise, too,' said the Kandy Man. 'I am a Kandy Man of my word.' He lumbered over to a large brown sack of ingredients and pulled out a heavy black shovel. 'But now our little bargain is over,' he said. 'It's time to kill you.' He moved slowly towards the Doctor.

The Doctor sighed heavily. 'Oh dear,' he groaned. 'I was afraid you might say that.' The Doctor took the soda siphon out of his jacket pocket. 'Ah well, here we go again,' he said, as he squirted lemonade over the feet of the advancing Kandy Man.

The chemical reaction was instantaneous – the Kandy Man once again found himself stuck to the kitchen floor.

He swung the shovel at the Doctor, but the Kandy Man's tormentor had already danced out of range.

'No!' bellowed the Kandy Man. He took aim and threw the shovel with all his considerable strength, but the Doctor caught it neatly above his head, and replaced it in the sack. Then the Kandy Man realized that Gilbert had left the kitchen. 'Gilbert?' he said softly. 'Gilbert!' he screamed. But the only person who heard him was the Doctor, who doffed his hat and quietly slipped through the doorway.

Daisy K had wasted no time marching Ace and Susan Q to the Happiness Patrol's headquarters, and they now stood, dishevelled and exhausted, in front of the immaculately groomed Helen A. Daisy K stood behind them, her gun trained on the prisoners, and Joseph C stood to one side, looking rather embarrassed.

Helen A seemed to be in a good mood. 'Just now I was lucky enough to see your cabaret act,' she told Ace and Susan. Her tone hardened. 'I hated it,' She paused for effect. 'But you were lucky too.'

Ace had taken enough of the way that Helen A played games with people. 'I'm not frightened of you,' she said through gritted teeth. 'You or your pet ferret!'

Helen A continued calmly, ignoring Ace's outburst. 'And so you'll be giving your performance again, for the very last time, at the Forum late show tonight.'

'I'm nobody's performing dog,' said Ace, 'not yours, not nobody's.'

This time Helen A was rattled. 'That, Ace Sigma,' she snarled, 'is just where you're wrong.' She snapped her fingers and Joseph hurried forward. He was carrying a big old-fashioned camera with an enormous flash bulb attached to it.

'A big smile, now, ladies!' he said, as he pointed the camera at them. Ace and Susan Q grimaced at the camera as the flashbulb exploded into light.

Wulfric and his small band of Pipe People were slowly coming to terms with the loss of Wences. Many of their number had been killed by predators or destroyed by the doompipe since they had been forced into the pipes. But they were determined to survive, so when they heard the scraping noise in the pipe near them they were ready for danger, weapons at the ready.

Wences crawled out of the shadows and collapsed at Wulfric's feet. Silently two of the Pipe People came forward and hoisted Wences on to their shoulders. The small group moved off towards a secret place where Wences could recover.

Fifi, a little way off in the darkness, noted the direction the solemn procession had taken, and then went back to licking her wounds.

There was no one around, but Earl didn't need an audience. He put the harmonica to his lips and blew a stream of soulful notes into the night air. Then he stopped playing, took off his hat, and put it down on the street in front of him. If someone did pass by and felt like contributing, he didn't want them to feel he wasn't grateful.

11

Earl had played five numbers before anyone came along. The man was wearing regulation pink overalls and carried a large poster and a bucket of paste. He did not seem to notice Earl or the music, but Earl quickly changed what he was playing to a particularly trite tune he had heard in an airport lounge on Earth. The man didn't look as if he belonged to the Happiness Patrol, but Earl had learnt that you couldn't be too careful.

He kept playing, and watched the man as he held the poster against the wall and spread paste over it. When he was satisfied that it was firmly stuck in place he replaced the brush in the bucket and walked away, continuing to ignore Earl.

Earl was still contemplating this episode when a familiar hat spun across the street and landed neatly next to his. It was closely followed by its owner, the Doctor, who produced a pair of spoons from deep inside his jacket and began to play them, improvising rhythms to Earl's music.

When they came to the end of the piece, the Doctor picked up both the hats and shook them ostentatiously. They were both empty.

'It's been a quiet night,' said Earl.

The Doctor gave Earl his trilby. 'It's been busy for me.'

'So what now?' asked Earl. He was sure the Doctor would have a plan.

'I've lost my friend, Ace,' the Doctor began, but his sentence trailed away as something caught his attention. Earl realized that the Doctor was looking at the poster that the sombre man had pasted on to the wall. It was a picture of two girls, both looking surprised. Underneath the picture, in big letters was the legend: 'Tonight at the Forum'. It was the photograph of Ace and Susan Q that Joseph C had taken in the Happiness Patrol's headquarters.

'But I think I know where I can find her,' said the Doctor, completing his sentence. Almost before he had finished speaking he was striding down the street with Earl hurrying after him. Within a few minutes they were hurrying across the Forum square, dwarfed by the imposing facade of the Forum itself. The Doctor, pursued by Earl, headed for the stage door tucked in the corner of the square. He had a few more questions for the taciturn doorman.

Ernest P was asleep when they arrived and didn't take kindly to being woken by the Doctor's rapping on the small glass window. He looked more grouchy than usual by the time he emerged.

The Doctor didn't have time for pleasantries. 'When's the show?' he asked.

'In five minutes,' grunted Ernest P, who hoped they would go away so he could go back to sleep. 'You'll catch it if you're quick.'

Earl was surprised. 'Five minutes?' he said incredulously. 'So why are the posters going up now?'

'Why not?' said Ernest P, retreating into his booth. 'They're just for show. We always have a full house because attendance is compulsory.'

'You mean you've got a captive audience,' said the Doctor grimly. He looked across the square and saw that a crowd had gathered near the main entrance of the Forum. They were being shepherded by the Happiness Patrol into an orderly queue. The Doctor saw that the guard in charge of the operation was none other than Prisclla P from the waiting zone. The Doctor pulled Earl into the safety of the shadows next to the stage door.

The crowd was the audience for the late show. Priscilla P was vetting them as they entered the building, just checking that they were really happy, that they really had a sunny outlook on the world, and that nobody was putting on a show for the benefit of the Happiness Patrol.

She stopped a middle-aged couple as they were going through the door. 'What's the definition of a polygon?' she asked them. The man and the woman looked blank. 'A dead parrot,' said Priscilla P, without a trace of humour. But this was obviously the funniest joke the couple had ever heard. They shrieked with laughter, and tears of merriment rolled down their cheeks. Priscilla P was pleased with this response. 'They're OK,' she said to the Happiness Patrol guard, who ushered them inside.

The next couple were young and, although smiling, looked pale and unhealthy. Priscilla P took an instant dislike to them. 'What's the definition of a parrot?' she asked, a mean look in her eye. The couple didn't reply. They just kept smiling. Priscilla moved towards them. 'A plane figure contained by more than four sides,' she intoned, and waited for their reaction. At first they didn't move, baffled by her words. But then the man began laughing, a wheezy laugh, rusty from lack of use. After a moment the woman joined in, laughing a high-pitched, eerie laugh. Priscilla P did not join in. 'It's not funny,' she said. 'You're faking.' She snapped her fingers. 'Take them away,' she ordered. Two guards moved in, grabbed the couple roughly and dragged them to a nearby van. Later, they would be taken to a remote part of the planet where they would become drones and put to work in the sugar factories.

The Doctor had seen enough of this. He turned to Earl, crouching next to him in the alcove. 'Go back to the demonstrators and bring them to the Forum,' he whispered.

'What if they don't want to come?'

'You'll find a way,' said the Doctor encouragingly. 'I'll meet you here.'

Keeping low, Earl sprinted across the square and disappeared down a narrow alleyway. The Doctor waited until the people in the queue had either gone into the Forum or been taken away in the van and the Happiness Patrol had dispersed. Then he went back to the stage door booth and rapped on the glass again. Ernest P dragged himself over to the window.

'I need to know if one of tonight's artistes is in the Forum yet,' demanded the Doctor.

'I'll just have a look at my list,' said Ernest P grudgingly. 'She's called Ace.'

Ernest P shuffled the papers on his table unenthusiastically. 'I can't do anything until I find my list, now, can I? I put it down here somewhere.'

The Doctor pulled his hat down over his eyes and squeezed to one side as three Happiness Patrol guards came down the passageway from the inside of the theatre. Two of them were dragging a body bag. The third carried a pot of paint. The Doctor watched as the procession went out through the stage door and came to a halt in front of a line of posters on the wall, most of which had been obliterated by pink paint. As two of the guards heaved the body bag into a waiting skip, the third splashed pink paint over one of the posters, a photograph of a young girl. When she had finished painting she pulled a thick, black crayon from a pocket in her tunic and scrawled RIP in large letters across the poster.

'Oh dear,' said Ernest P, who had found his list and was now watching the scene. 'Doesn't look as if Daphne S went down too well, does it?'

The Doctor didn't reply. He was staring at the poster at the end of the line, the only one which had not been defaced with the letters RIP. It was the poster of Ace and Susan Q.

Ernest consulted his clipboard. 'Ace Sigma, wasn't it?' he said.

'That's right.'

He ran his pencil down the list. 'What does she do then, this Ace Sigma?'

'Do?'

Ernest P ran through the litany of possibilities. 'Sing, dance, juggle, magic, vent or impressions?'

The Doctor remembered Ace's remarkable facility with a can of nitro-nine. 'She makes things disappear,' he ventured.

'Magic,' said Ernest P, going back to his list.

'There's nothing magical about the way she does it,' said the Doctor, to no one in particular.

Ernest P was shaking his head in an exaggerated manner. 'Nothing down here under magic,' he said, with obvious pleasure. 'But I can do you an Ace Sigma on a miracle survival act.'

'What's that?' asked the Doctor. But he stopped Ernest before he could reply. 'No,' he said, 'let me guess. It will be a miracle if she survives.'

The Doctor's fears, however, were slightly premature. Ace and Susan Q, although they were approaching the Forum escorted by Daisy K and a Happiness Patrol unit, had not yet arrived, and they were already planning their survival.

Susan Q was walking next to Ace, close enough to whisper to her without being overheard by Daisy K. 'As long as you're looking cute, you have a chance.'

'Cute!' sad Ace, loudly enough to earn her a prod in the back from one of the Happiness Patrol guards. She prided herself on getting this far in life without looking cute, and she wasn't planning to start now.

'Big smiles, girls!' It was Daisy K, sneering at them. 'Showtime soon!'

Susan Q whispered again to Ace. 'Don't give up. We might get through this alive.'

They passed under an archaic speaker, decorated with baroque curls. It was spewing out an arrangement of an old pop song, the angular tune submerged under a sea of strings so that it lost all its original bite.

'I hate that music,' said Ace.

'You're not the only one,' winced Susan Q.

A single shot rang out and the music stopped as the

speaker flew off the wall and landed in the street in front of them. 'A sniper!' barked Daisy K, as Ace and Susan cheered the marksmanship. 'Get down! Lucy O! Jane M! Covering fire! The rest of you – go for that sniper!'

The sniper attacking the Happiness Patrol unit was a drone that had stumbled across David S's gun after the Doctor had thrown it over the balcony. He knew he would eventually be overpowered, but he was looking for some revenge before the end.

The Happiness Patrol unit split into sections, according to the paragraph in the training manual headed: 'Ambush, from above'. Several dropped into shooting positions with overhead cover and delivered covering fire for those mounting the attack on the sniper's balcony. Daisy, unseen by everyone except Ace, crept away from the danger, looking for a safe hiding place.

Ace and Susan Q, crouching by the wall, suddenly discovered they were no longer guarded. Ace turned to Susan. 'Are you thinking what I'm thinking?'

'People get killed thinking like that.'

Ace snorted. 'People get killed anyway,' she said.

They waited for a few moments, until they were sure no one was watching. 'Now!' said Ace, and they ran up a narrow alley, away from the street. The sniper was still firing down on the Happiness Patrol, and their escape went unnoticed in the confusion.

Ace saw a dark, dingy doorway ahead. They could hide in there for a moment and work out the best plan of action. 'In here,' Ace shouted to Susan Q, a few paces behind her. They darted in and collapsed against the wall, breathing heavily. But they weren't alone in the doorway. Daisy K had chosen it as her hiding place. She smiled and raised her fun gun. Ace and Susan Q slowly put their hands on their heads.

Ace hated Daisy K for her cowardice. 'Face-ache,' she said with contempt. But Daisy just kept smiling. She was the one with the gun.

The sniper had died in a volley of Happiness Patrol

bullets. He had been left hanging over the balcony as a warning to others, and Ace tried not to look at him as the unit reassembled. It did not seem to affect Susan in the same way, and she was already working on their best chance of survival. Ace assumed that living on Terra Alpha had hardened Susan Q against the sights and sounds of this vicious regime.

'Remember,' whispered Susan Q urgently, 'flutter your eyelashes, and lots of teeth in your smile.'

But Ace was angry. 'I'd rather lob something at them.'

'And remember to use your dimples,' continued Susan, undeterred.

'I'd use more than my dimples,' growled Ace.

'Quiet!' barked Daisy K, as she brought the butt of her fun gun sharply down on the back of Ace's head.

12

The drones were approaching Forum Square. They were all dressed in black, and most of them wore bowler hats, with black veils covering their faces. They marched in time to a slow drumbeat. Earl was at the head of the procession, playing his harmonica, weaving a bluesy dirge around the constant beat of the drums.

Helen A watched this scene on the television monitor in her suite, occasionally looking down to stroke Fifi, sitting in her lap. After careful consideration Fifi had decided not to attack the Pipe People, and had used her remaining strength to crawl out of a manhole next to the palace doors, where she had collapsed. Helen A had found Fifi and taken her to the best doctors on Terra Alpha, where she had been given the sort of medical care only the richest Alphans could ever hope for. To the great delight of Helen A, Fifi had recovered. Her pet was heavily bandaged, but she had just heard from the doctors that the bandages were ready to come off. The news, however, had been spoilt for her by the sight of the drones' miserable procession.

'Look at them, Fifi,' she said, as she unfastened the safety pin on one of the largest bandages. 'Dreary clothes, turgid music and terrible deportment. They're just so depressing.' She felt her spirits sinking and knew she couldn't watch any longer. She flicked a switch on a remote control unit and the picture disappeared. She twisted a microphone towards her and composed herself before she spoke.

'Happiness will prevail,' she announced into the microphone. 'Happiness Patrol section B, prepare to effect a large scale disappearance. A drone demonstration is moving towards Forum Square. Proceed there directly. Take no prisoners. Summary executions for all drones, including the Sigma musician.'

She picked up the remote control unit and pointed it at the television set. She selected a new channel and the room was filled with the sound of canned laughter. Helen A squealed with delight as she watched the programme, an old situation comedy imported from Earth. A man with no trousers was being chased round a sofa by a middle-aged woman, when the sitting-room door opened to reveal the vicar.

'That's better, isn't it, my darling?' said Helen A, gathering up Fifi in her arms.

She could hear alarms going off in the building and the familiar sounds of pounding feet as section B of the Happiness Patrol mustered to destroy the drones. 'I can already feel my spirits lifting,' said Helen A.

The show was just finishing as Helen A removed the last of Fifi's bandages, rolling them round her hand as they came off. 'And the last one,' she said, as she gently peeled away the one remaining strip of linen. She was pleased with what she saw. Fifi was looking as fit and sleek as she had ever seen her. She had lost some fur, but that would grow again. Fifi, too, was enjoying the newfound sense of freedom now that the constricting bandages had been removed. She stretched her muscles. The small spikes, normally concealed in the fur on the top of her head, sprung into an upright position. She curled her lip and snarled, long and low. She was ready for hunting again.

'There we are,' said Helen A, smoothing down the remaining fur, 'all mended.' She found that talking to Fifi came easily to her, much more easily than to Joseph C or any of her subordinates in the Happiness Patrol, most of whom she despised and certainly didn't trust. She looked into the eyes of the Stigorax.

101

'We're a team, Fifi, you and I. We look after each other. And we will make this a happy planet, in spite of the bunglers and killjoys that surround us. If they're miserable, then we'll put them out of their misery. After all, it's for their own good.'

Helen A's eyes were bright with excitement. 'But first of all,' she said, 'a bit of harmless revenge. You take the vermin in the pipe. I'll take the vermin at the Forum.'

Fifi growled softly in anticipation.

The Doctor had at last discovered from Ernest P that Ace and Susan Q had not yet been brought to the Forum for their turn in the late show. He knew that Earl would be bringing the drones here, so he had decided to sit on the main steps of the Forum and await developments. A large loudspeaker was attached to the facade of the Forum, and the Doctor was grateful for the regular news bulletins which kept him up to date about events.

The speaker crackled into life. 'This is a public happiness announcement,' said the voice of the anonymous newscaster. 'A depression is moving towards Forum Square. Stay clear of the area. The proper authorities will restore harmony. Happiness will prevail.'

The Doctor knew only too well that this message referred to the drones and the measures Helen A was taking to destroy them. But he had no intention of leaving. He was curious to see what would happen now that the Happiness Patrol was arriving – and of course, he had a plan.

He took a close look at the square while he waited. At the top of the steps, a few feet away from him, there was a free-standing microphone, presumably used by Helen A to address the public, which he was sure she did with monotonous regularity. But apart from that, it was a bare, empty sort of place. The Doctor could just about make out murals of grotesquely smiling creatures on the walls of the Forum and the surrounding buildings. But the paint had peeled and the colours faded. It reminded him of Earth – specifically of Venice in the late twentieth century, before it slid slowly into the sea. And then the Doctor understood that here was a society in decay, playing out its last act. This comforted him, and he resolved to do whatever he could to make that last act as quick and painless as possible.

His musings were interrupted by Trevor Sigma, who wandered into the square with a large roll of paper under his arm.

'Hello, Trevor,' the Doctor greeted him. 'Come to see the fun? Or is that classified information?'

But Trevor seemed more relaxed than before. 'No, Doctor,' he said. 'I'm leaving this planet.' He waved the roll of paper. 'I've completed my census.' He unrolled the end, pulled a pen from the inside of his jacket, and made a few brief notes.

'Where's the Galactic Census Bureau sending you next?' asked the Doctor.

'Earth. Been there?'

'Once or twice,' said the Doctor wistfully.

'Miserable sort of place,' said Trevor.

The Doctor nodded his head in agreement. 'You're making me feel nostalgic,' he said.

He picked up the end of Trevor's roll of paper, and idly read what was written there. It seemed to be a list of names. 'Wait a minute,' he said, scanning the list eagerly. 'Silas P, Harold V. I know these names.' He remembered Harold V at the one-armed bandit, and the crack of the Happiness Patrol guns moments after he had left Silas sitting on the bench. Silas, although working for Helen A, was just as much a victim of her regime as Harold. He turned back to Trevor. 'You can't give these names to the bureau. They may have lived here once but . . .'

Trevor interrupted him. 'They've disappeared. I know. Strange, isn't it? Don't ask me why, but that's what the bureau wants.'

'A list of the disappeared?'

'That's right.'

But the Doctor knew why. The bureau had obviously heard about recent events on Terra Alpha and, no doubt after countless committee meetings, had decided to send Trevor to gather information. His findings would be analysed, and after a further series of meetings a decision would be taken to do something about it. The only snag was that by the time any action was taken, no one on Terra Alpha, if the planet still existed, would remember anything about Helen A or the Happiness Patrol.

Still, that didn't make the size of Trevor's list of the disappeared any less horrific. 'When were you last on Terra Alpha?' the Doctor asked him.

'Let me see,' said Trevor, 'In Alphan time, six months ago.'

So all these Alphans had disappeared in the last six months. The Doctor held one end of the roll of paper firmly and threw the roll across the square. As it unrolled, the paper, covered in Trevor's tiny, neat writing, cascaded down the steps, right across the square, and into an adjoining street before the Doctor, peering into the distance, finally saw the other end.

Fifi was sprawled across one of the most comfortable chairs in Helen A's suite, resting before going back down into the pipes to hunt the Pipe People, when Helen A walked briskly into the room with a leash made of strong metal links.

'Walkies!' cried Helen A brightly. In an instant Fifi was by her side, getting increasingly animated as Helen A clipped on the leash. As they set off for the execution yard, where Helen A had arranged to meet Joseph C, Wences watched from behind a ventilation grille set low into the wall. He scampered away down the pipe to the other Pipe People to warn them to get ready to fight for their lives.

Joseph C was sauntering round the execution yard, breathing in the night air, when Helen A arrived with Fifi. He slid the manhole cover aside and took the leash from Helen when she unclipped it. She gently lowered Fifi into the manhole and they both watched with pride as Fifi sniffed the air and set off in search of her prey.

Helen liked the yard at this time of night, when the last execution had taken place – or not taken place in the case of today. But even that recollection did not stop her taking pleasure from the peace and quiet of the secluded space. She slipped her hand through Joseph's arm and they walked slowly around the yard, listening to the sounds of the night.

Tonight was rather noisy, as section B set off in pursuit of the drones. Just after Helen had released Fifi, she heard the tell-tale ice-cream-van music of one of the Happiness Patrol jeeps passing close by the yard on its way to Forum Square. It was being driven by a rather grumpy Gilbert M, whose bad mood was partly because he was a scientist and resented being press-ganged into helping the Happiness Patrol just because they had an emergency on their hands, and partly because he was fed up to the back teeth of the warmongering screams coming from Priscilla P in the passenger seat.

'Over there!' shrieked Priscilla P, pointing at a shape in the road.

'What?' grunted Gilbert, not even attempting to disguise the anger in his voice.

'A killjoy – in the shadows. Dark coat, drooping shoulders, a tear glistening on his cheek. 'Summary execution?' she asked hopefully.

'Not this time, Priscilla,' groaned Gilbert. 'Save it for the drones.'

The Doctor was strolling backwards and forwards across the top of the Forum steps, twiddling his thumbs and glancing every now and then at his watch. He knew how fast Ace walked, where she was coming from, and roughly when she had left, and was trying to estimate her arrival time. When he had done this he hunted around for something else to keep him occupied – it was then that he noticed the microphone. He walked back and forth several times more before he decided to do it. After checking that there was no one about, he tapped the microphone to test it, and then took it off its stand.

After a final check that he was alone, he held the microphone close to his mouth and sang.

'It's still the same old story,' crooned the Doctor, 'a fight for love and glory, a case of do or die.'

It wasn't a pleasant sound. He frowned at the microphone and replaced it in the stand. 'Perhaps not,' he said to no one in particular. And then he heard the final notes of the tune drifting across the square, answering his singing. It was the familiar haunting tone of the harmonica.

'Earl!' said the Doctor, as the musician bounded up the steps towards him.

'The drones are on their way,' said Earl, pocketing his harmonica.

'Thank you, Earl,' said the Doctor. 'It's all falling nicely into place. As time goes by,' he added. Earl laughed at the Doctor's reference to the song.

The Doctor was already working out just exactly who he was expecting. 'We've got Ace arriving first, with her guards, of course, and you're bringing the drones, which only leaves the Happiness Patrol section sent by Helen A to make us all disappear in the nastiest possible way.'

Earl didn't know that there was going to be such a party. 'Sounds complicated,' he said.

'Nonsense,' said the Doctor, 'it's simplicity itself. But you have to help me – and you'll have to get the time just right.'

'What sort of time would you like, Doctor?' asked Earl, producing the harmonica. 'How about this?' He played a snatch of music.

'Play it by ear, Earl,' said the Doctor.

As Earl ran down the steps and out of the square to fetch the drones, the Doctor pulled out his pocket watch and consulted it. 'Now,' he said to himself. A few moments later, Daisy K led Ace, Susan Q and the Happiness Patrol unit into the square. The Doctor stepped up to the microphone. 'You're late,' he said.

'Doctor!' shouted Ace. Although she was relieved to see

him again, she had always had a feeling that he would turn up sooner or later.

'You've no idea how happy I am to see you, Ace,' said the Doctor, his voice booming round the square and echoing from the buildings opposite the Forum.

'Sorry to keep you, Doctor,' said Daisy, her voice full of mock sincerity, 'But now it's funtime!'

The Happiness Patrol formed into firing squad formation at the bottom of the steps, aiming up at the Doctor. 'Have a nice death, Doctor,' grinned Daisy K, her teeth picking out the light from a nearby streetlamp.

The Doctor was defenceless. Ace was worried. 'Doctor!' she shouted, urging him to make a run for it.

But the Doctor seemed nonchalant as ever. 'It's all right, Ace,' he called down to her, moving away from the microphone. 'They can't fire. Because they see before them a happy man,' he chuckled, smiling broadly for the benefit of the Happiness Patrol. 'And their logic will tell them, twisted as it is, that as such they have no power over me.'

The Doctor was right. The members of the firing squad, who could follow his reasoning but had never thought about it before, were confused. Some lowered their weapons. Others looked to Daisy K for guidance, but she appeared to be as confused as the rest of them.

'Of course,' continued the Doctor, 'some days I may feel a little grouchy perhaps, a wee bit bad-tempered . . .'

The Happiness Patrol saw a glimmer of hope and raised their weapons into the firing position again. But the Doctor was only teasing. '. . . but today isn't one of those days.' He watched the guns lower once more. 'Because today,' he ended triumphantly, grinning from ear to ear, 'the Doctor and the drones are having a ball!'

As he spoke, right on cue, Earl led the drones into the Forum Square. Ace had seen their gloomy procession earlier in the evening and watched in amazement as they threw off their black cloaks and jackets to reveal pink working dungarees, and started dancing and clapping to the lively jig Earl was playing on his harmonica.

107

Watching this, Daisy K and the Happiness Patrol unit began to look even more depressed – the drones were protected by their happiness. In short, everyone was having a good time except the members of the Happiness Patrol.

The festivities in the square were now interrupted by the arrival of the convoy of jeeps, including the one driven by Gilbert M, carrying the guards of section B of the Happiness Patrol, with their orders to wipe out the drones. The jeeps screeched to a halt and the guards jumped out and lined up before the drones, who were now doing a conga up and down the Forum's steps.

The Doctor rushed back to the microphone when he saw the guards preparing their fun guns. 'You can't do it, Happiness Patrol section B,' he told them. 'You can't go down in the history of the galaxy as a bunch of party-poopers.' He waved towards Daisy K's forlorn unit, standing to one side of the square. 'The only killjoys in this square,' he said, 'are behind you!' He watched with satisfaction as section B turned as one woman on their miserable colleagues. 'Look at them!' cried the Doctor, beginning to enjoy the pleasures of oratory, 'Wretched, snivelling creatures, wallowing in their own . . .' The Doctor couldn't think of the word.

'Weltschmerz!' cried a voice from one of the cars. It was Gilbert M, who wouldn't have missed this for the world.

The Doctor waved his thanks. 'Wallowing in their own Weltschmerz,' he announced, rolling the word round his mouth. Section B advanced on the hapless unit. 'All except Ace and Susan Q, of course,' added the Doctor quickly, 'who are very glad to see me.' Ace and Susan Q laughed deliriously, and ran unchallenged through the ranks of the Happiness Patrol. In the confusion Ace even managed to knock Daisy K's gun out of her hands. 'And I'm happy they're glad,' said the Doctor, as they joined him at the top of the steps.

From their vantage point, the Doctor, Ace and Susan Q watched section B form a circle round Daisy K and her guards. 'No!' screamed Daisy K. 'Stop! That's an order!'

But the circle, keenly led by Priscilla, continued to close in until they had overcome the resistance of Daisy K's unit and arrested all the guards, including Daisy herself.

The Doctor's attention, however, was soon elsewhere. He had noticed an unattended jeep standing beside the stage door, and ran down the steps towards it, shouting to Ace and Susan Q to follow him. 'Into the jeep!' he yelled. They all dived in and the Doctor tried to work out how to start it. Ace saw that they had been spotted trying to escape by Happiness Patrol guards, who were running towards them.

'Come on, Professor,' she urged, 'get this heap of junk moving!'

'Nice to have you back, Ace,' said the Doctor, as the jeep burst into life, swerving away from the pursuing guards. The Doctor headed out of the square, slowing down only to allow Earl to hurl himself into the back seat next to Susan Q.

Now that all the active service Happiness Patrol units were deployed at Forum Square, the streets around the execution yard were quiet. Helen A strolled round the yard with Joseph C, listening to the soft muzak flowing out of a tiny concealed speaker. She was glad that she had delegated duties at the late show to Daisy K.

'Lovely evening,' she said softly to Joseph C.

'Yes, dear,' he agreed.

'The sort of evening that makes you happy to be alive.' There was no reply. 'I said the sort of evening that makes you feel happy to be alive.' This time her voice had a steely edge to it.

'Yes, dear,' said Joseph again, without enthusiasm. 'I'm glad you're happy,' he added for good measure.

'And I'm happy you're glad,' replied Helen A, softened by his concern.

This Alphan idyll was rudely disturbed by loud, crackling interference on the speaker, which obliterated the muzak. The static subsided, to be replaced by a newsflash. Helen A and Joseph C stopped walking and listened.

'Happiness will prevail,' said the newscaster. 'Chaos in Forum Square. Fighting has broken out in the ranks of the Happiness Patrol itself. Happiness will . . .' The voice faded into a loud burst of static. Soon the muzak was playing again.

Helen A stormed round the yard, walking off her fury. 'However hard I try,' she ranted at Joseph, 'however much work I put in, something always happens.' Joseph shifted uncomfortably. He hated her moods but he knew that any conciliatory noises he tried to make would only inflame the situation. 'Even moments like this aren't sacred,' raved Helen A. She suddenly spun round to face Joseph. 'But one day we'll live in harmony,' she said. 'One day I will be appreciated.'

'Yes, dear,' said Joseph lamely.

'Here,' said Helen A. She handed him the leash which had been wrapped loosely round her wrist. 'You wait for Fifi. I shall obviously have to deal with this myself.'

'Yes, dear.'

Helen A paused before leaving the yard to gather her strength for the battle ahead. In the distance she heard the unmistakable sound of Fifi howling, the sound she made when she was closing on her prey. At least someone is doing her job properly, thought Helen A.

The Doctor slammed on the brakes and the jeep juddered to a halt. They were in a deserted street, silent apart from the distinctive tinkle of muzak from a speaker set high on the wall.

'Here we are,' said the Doctor, jumping out. The others followed him and he led them to a manhole in the middle of the street. Ace helped him remove the cover.

'So where are we going, Professor?' she asked.

'To the top,' said the Doctor, jumping down the hole.

When they were all in the pipe, the Doctor asked them to be quiet and they listened. They waited a minute, two minutes – longer. And then they heard what the Doctor was listening for. It was the low, almost beautiful sound of Fifi's howl. 'Come on,' said the Doctor, and strode off down the pipe, leading them in the direction of the noise.

Fifi had picked up the scent of the Pipe People shortly after she had been released down the pipe in the execution yard. Tracking them along the pipes, she could have already made a kill several times. But she was in no hurry. She didn't enjoy surprise ambushes: she preferred to wear her quarry down, to see the desperation in exhausted eyes before she moved in for the kill.

But the Pipe People weren't ready to give in yet. Wulfric was leading them from the front, refusing to show any sign of weariness, as they scampered down the pipes trying to shake Fifi off their trail. But they had lost their way and were in pipes that they didn't recognize. Hearing Fifi's howls getting closer and closer they took one turning, then, guessing, took another. Suddenly they were faced with a brick wall. The pipe had been closed off.

They were in a dead end.

The howls grew louder. Out of the corner of his eye, Wences saw movements in the shadows. He spun round, his spear raised, ready for throwing.

The Doctor and his party stepped out of the darkness.

'Doctor!' said Wulfric in amazement.

The Doctor doffed his hat. 'Wulfric, Wences.' They heard Fifi howl again. She now sounded very close. 'It's a Stigorax,' said the Doctor. 'Extremely intelligent, ruthless predators.'

'Danger!' said Wences urgently.

'Fifi!' explained Wulfric.

In the jeep Ace had been boasting of her exploits in the pipe with a can of nitro-nine. The Doctor turned to her. 'Ace, this wouldn't be Fifi, as in Fifi the annoying rat who you claim to have blown to smithereens.'

Ace shrugged. 'Nobody's perfect, Professor.'

'Yes,' sighed the Doctor. 'Including Fifi.' He indicated a small side-tunnel with the end of his umbrella, the entrance of which was concealed behind a wall of encrusted sugar and so had been invisible to the Pipe People. 'This way I think,' he said.

'That way,' said Wences, looking alarmed.

Wulfric was shaking his head. 'Danger!' he said.

But the Doctor just smiled. 'Precisely,' he said. They all followed him into the pipe.

Daisy K was reluctantly playing the one-armed bandit in the waiting zone. After a few failures, she decided she had had enough of this ridiculous charade and turned to Priscilla P, who was standing over her, fun gun at the ready.

'Keep playing!' barked Priscilla P. 'Enjoy yourself!'

Daisy K turned back to the game. 'Strictly speaking, Priscilla P,' she said, as she pulled the handle, 'this game is for killjoys. And I am not a killjoy.'

But Priscilla P was unmoved. 'I spent five years hunting down killjoys.'

'Yes, I know, Priscilla,' said Daisy, trying to be patient. 'I was your squad leader. I am not a killjoy.'

Priscilla P enjoyed talking about her years at the sharp end. 'You pick up a lot on the streets,' she said. 'You can see it in their eyes – feel their fear. They know you're watching them.'

The monitor on the one-armed bandit flickered into life and the familiar face of Helen A appeared.

'Ignore it,' ordered Priscilla P. 'It's just a recording.'

But on the monitor Helen A took exception to this. 'It is not just a recording, Priscilla P,' she said sternly. 'I am transmitting live.' Priscilla P looked at the screen suspiciously, wondering if it was some kind of trick. 'Put down your gun and release Daisy K,' said the image of Helen A.

'But she's a killjoy,' protested Priscilla. 'I arrested her myself.'

'I'm losing my patience,' said Helen A testily. 'Release Daisy K. I need her at the palace.'

Priscilla P finally capitulated. 'What shall I do, ma'am?' she asked the one-armed bandit.

'You're in the waiting zone,' said Helen A slowly and deliberately, as if explaining something to a child, 'so wait.' And with that the screen went blank.

Priscilla P stared long and hard at Daisy K before she eventually lowered her gun. She snapped it open and began to take it apart. She didn't like being told to stay in the waiting zone, not when there were killjoys on the loose, but at least her gun needed an overhaul.

Daisy K took longer than necessary to get back to the palace. She knew that Helen A would want her version of events in Forum Square and needed time to work out her story.

She was further unnerved by Helen A's small-talk as they waited for tea to arrive. The weather, the economy, even the state of Alphan stumpball – a combination of cricket and baseball whose rules Daisy K had never mastered. Only when the tea was before them, and Helen A was pouring it into two cups, did she raise the question of the night's events. But things had moved on. Helen A had received alarming reports from the outlying areas of Terra Alpha. So when she finally turned her attention to the crisis, her first question took Daisy K completely by surprise.

'Tell me, Daisy K,' she said pleasantly. 'when the Happiness Patrol got together with the drones and decided to form a wrecking gang to dismantle the sugar factories, what were you doing at the time? Just interested,' she smiled.

This development was news to Daisy K, but she thought better of betraying any surprise to Helen A. 'I was under armed guard,' she said.

'Priscilla P?'

'Yes.'

'Ah.' Helen A offered Daisy K a biscuit. 'It's just that I thought you were equipped with a high-velocity fun gun, that's all.'

Daisy K knew she would have to tell Helen the truth. 'It

113

was knocked out of my hands by one of the prisoners in Forum Square.'

'One of the prisoners?' asked Helen A. She wanted to hear the girl's name.

'Ace Sigma,' said Daisy K.

'Ace Sigma. I wondered when she would turn up to haunt me again.' She glanced up at Daisy. 'Not that I mind, you understand.'

'Of course not,' said Daisy K, hastily.

'A charming girl in so many ways,' said Helen A wistfully. She poured Daisy K another cup of tea. She put the teapot down and was lost in thought for several moments. Daisy remained silent. After a while Helen A jumped up and paced briskly round the room, suddenly more businesslike than before.

'So,' said Helen A as she walked, 'what are we left with after this little local difficulty in Forum Square? Remind me.'

Daisy K quickly assimilated the new information she had just learnt. 'A posse heading out to the sugar factories, and the Doctor and his gang roaming the city.'

'Well,' said Helen brightly, 'nothing insoluble there. The factories are heavily defended and we'll soon track down the Doctor.'

'He may have gone down into the pipes,' warned Daisy K.

But this news seemed to cheer Helen. 'Excellent,' she said. 'Then we'll leave Fifi to deal with him.'

The Doctor was striding along the pipes at the head of his party, attempting to lead them away from Fifi, but they could still hear her eerie moans. The pipes, however, distorted the sound and there was no way of telling how near she was. At one moment the cry would seem so distant they could hardly make it out; at the next it would sound as if she were waiting round the next twist in the pipe. The only thing of which they could be certain was that she hadn't lost the trail.

114

They were now making their way through a low-hanging canopy of sugar stalactites. The Pipe People, suffering from tiredness and hunger, paused every few moments to eat to restore their strength. As the Doctor ducked under a particularly large stalactite his umbrella accidentally caught the end of it, and gave out a long, ringing note.

'What was that?' asked Ace.

'Sounded like an A-flat,' said Earl, who had nearly perfect pitch.

The Doctor turned to them and pressed his finger to his lips. 'Quiet!' he whispered. He stopped and studied the mass of stalactities hanging over their heads.

'Why are we whispering?' whispered Susan Q.

'I'll tell her,' said Earl, who remembered the Doctor's explanation when he had asked the same question. 'Crystallized syrup,' he told Susan Q. 'It becomes unstable as it ages.'

Ace thought about this. 'So a loud noise could set off a cave-in,' she said with relish.

'Not quite, Ace,' said the Doctor. 'It has to be the right noise.' But Ace had given him an idea.

A hundred yards behind them, crouching in the shadows, Fifi was watching their deliberations with interest. Her eyes glowed as she crawled towards them.

The Doctor, however, knew that Fifi would be watching them, and was setting a trap using himself and the others as bait. They waited in silence, as Fifi edged towards them, all of her senses working to the full. As she moved, one of the horns on her head clipped off the end of one of the stalactites, which rattled as it landed on the floor of the pipe. It was the signal the Doctor had been waiting for. He held up his umbrella and tapped the sugar crystal, which once again produced the ringing sound.

'Crucial,' said Ace.

'Yes,' said the Doctor grimly. 'It is crucial. Now get back, Ace – wait at the end of the pipe.' He directed her away from the mass of stalactites.

'Oh, come on Doctor,' complained Ace.

But the Doctor was firm. 'And take Susan Q and the Pipe People with you.' Ace didn't move. 'Now!' said the Doctor, forgetting to whisper.

Ace grudgingly moved off down the pipe, shepherding the others. The Doctor turned to Earl. 'Give me an A-flat,' he said.

Earl didn't understand. 'Eh?'

'No,' said the Doctor. 'A-flat.'

'Why?'

The Doctor raised his eyes heavenwards. Why, at moments of crisis, did people always want explanations. Very well, he thought, if that's what Earl wanted, that's what he would get.

'Resonance, Earl,' he said. 'Sympathetic vibration.' Earl looked blank. 'Aren't you familiar with Doctor John Wallace's paper to the Royal Society in 1677?' Earl nodded less than convincingly. The Doctor had had enough of this. 'Play, Earl!' he commanded.

The Doctor struck the crystal again and Earl produced the harmonica and played an A-flat. The discordant sound told them that Earl's note was a semi-tone too low. 'Wrong note,' said the Doctor. As he spoke a third note joined the chord – that of Fifi's howl. The Doctor peered down the pipe. He could just make out the sleek outline of Fifi as she stealthily approached them, preparing to pounce.

'Give me an A!' he ordered Earl, and he struck the crystal again. Earl changed the position of his hands and the note on the harmonica crept up until it blended with the noise coming from the crystal. But now, out of the corner of his eye, Earl had seen Fifi. He stopped playing.

'Isn't this dangerous?' he said.

'Of course it is,' said the Doctor. 'Keep playing.'

Earl put the harmonica back to his mouth and started playing again. The Doctor tapped the crystal once more. Fifi threw back her head and howled. But then, far above them, they heard a soft rumble, getting louder and louder, as the vibrations of the two notes started to work. The walls started shaking as the rumbling sound intensified. The

Doctor grabbed Earl and they both fled towards Ace and the Pipe People and safety.

Fifi chose this as the moment for her kill. She hurled herself towards them, baring her fangs and snarling. But she was too late. She was under the mass of stalactites just as the first one fell into the pipe. Within seconds she was buried, as one stalactite after another pounded down on top of her.

The Doctor, now reunited with the others, shielded his eyes from the dust blown up by the cave-in. They listened to Fifi's piteous cries getting softer and softer, until they finally stopped altogether.

Far away, someone else heard the cave-in. Joseph C was still walking round the execution yard, carrying Fifi's leash and waiting for her return. He was humming one of Helen A's favourite tunes to himself. When he heard the strange subterranean rumbling he stopped for a moment and listened. After a while, when things were quiet again, he continued his stroll and picked up his humming from where he had left off.

When the Doctor was satisfied that the avalanche was well and truly over, he assembled his bedraggled party and told them his plans. He now knew that his task was to dismantle the machinery of Helen A's regime, to remove the teeth from the monster. He gave Earl and Susan Q clear instructions on how to find the waiting zone and Priscilla P, and told them what to do when they arrived. In the meantime, he would take Ace back to the Kandy Kitchen. He was relying on the expertise of the Pipe People to guide him there.

They trudged down the pipe away from the sugary rubble. At the next manhole cover Earl and Susan Q were hoisted up into the street above and disappeared into the darkness. The Doctor's group, led by Wulfric, continued along the pipe. If their arrival in the Kandy Kitchen was to contain any element of surprise, they had to travel there underground.

Earl was impressed by the clarity of the Doctor's mental

map of the city of Terra Alpha. His instructions had taken them along a series of deserted side-streets, well away from the main thoroughfares permanently monitored by the Happiness Patrol, and soon they had spotted Priscilla P, pacing back and forth in the waiting zone.

They watched her from the cover of a shop doorway. Priscilla P took ten paces towards them, then turned her back on them and took ten paces away. They watched her approach . . . eight, nine, ten. 'Now!' whispered Earl.

As soon as Priscilla turned her back on them again Susan Q sprinted out. Earl counted to thirty inside his head. When he knew that Susan Q would be in position, he reached inside his jacket and pulled out his harmonica.

One of the few comforts provided for the waiting zone guard was an archaic wireless, permanently tuned in to Helen A's light music channel. Now that Priscilla P had overhauled and cleaned her gun twice the only thing left for her to do, until Helen A summoned her for duty, was to listen to the music, which she enjoyed. But suddenly even that pleasure turned sour. The pleasant, uplifting music which the station always played had changed to the baleful, mournful sound of a single harmonica, bending the sad notes as she listened. She was seduced for a moment, but then came to her senses and ran over to the wireless to switch it off.

The sad music played on.

The hairs on the back of Priscilla P's neck stood on end as she smelt danger. She realized that the music was not coming from the wireless but from a real instrument. She listened carefully, and tried to work out where the killjoy musician was hidden. The music seemed to be coming from nearby, specifically from the shop doorway just outside the waiting zone. Her finger curled round the trigger of her gun as she moved quietly towards the doorway. But Susan Q was already behind her. In one movement, she slipped a knotted scarf over Priscilla P's head and pulled hard.

13

Helen A and Daisy K had finished their tea party and moved through into the control room of the Happiness Patrol's headquarters, from which they could more easily follow the development of events on the planet. They had already heard several reports of rioting and destruction in the outlying areas of the planet, as thousands of killjoys came out of hiding to join the army of drones and rebellious Happiness Patrol guards.

The soft muzak was doing nothing to calm the nerves of Daisy, who was pacing round the room, pounding her fist into her open hand. Helen A, however, sitting in a comfortable chair away from the control desk, seemed to be completely unruffled by what was happening. She contemplated Daisy pacing back and forth. 'You seem agitated, Daisy K.'

Helen A's coolness only added to Daisy K's nerves. 'It's crumbling around us, isn't it?' she snapped. Why couldn't Helen A realize the seriousness of the situation, she thought angrily to herself.

'Not unhappy about something, I hope?' asked Helen A solicitously.

Daisy K quickly reminded her self that on no account must she seem depressed. 'No,' she said, forcing a smile.

'Good,' said Helen A, relaxing again. 'Because when the Doctor is picked up and brought in I don't want there to be anything for him to smile about.'

The muzak gave way to yet another newscast. 'Happiness will prevail,' said the newscaster.

'Get on with it,' said Daisy K, but not loudly enough for Helen A to hear.

The newscaster continued. 'We have just heard that the Happiness Patrol Section guarding the Nirvana sugar beet works in sector six has joined the growing band of vigilantes in the destruction of the factory. No news yet of the whereabouts of the Doctor.' He signed off and the muzak began again. Daisy K sat at the controls and drummed her fingers on the desk.

'It's just one factory, Daisy K,' said Helen calmly. 'I have built over a thousand.'

'And what about reports of riots and public unhappiness,' asked Daisy K, trying to sound as reasonable as possible.

'Simple,' smiled Helen. 'We need someone who knows the streets like the back of her hand, someone who is a good fighter, and above all, someone who is fiercely loyal.' She paused before saying, 'Priscilla P, perhaps.'

Daisy K hadn't forgotten her treatment at the hands of Priscilla P. 'She's a fanatic,' she said.

But Helen A would not be overruled. 'That's how I like them' she said. 'Get me the waiting zone.'

Daisy K pressed a button on the console, and a picture of the waiting zone flickered on to the monitor before them.

'What!' shouted Helen A, astonished at what she saw. For sure enough, there was Priscilla P. But far from being ready and willing to rid Helen A of this turbulent Doctor, she was quite helpless, gagged and bound at the hands and feet. As the automatic security camera swept across the rest of the waiting zone, it revealed the figure of Susan Q standing over Priscilla P, guarding her with her own fun gun. And finally, to complete their mortification, Earl Sigma came into view, a stream of melancholy notes issuing from the harmonica pressed to his mouth. Helen A had seen enough. She stormed over to the console and slammed down her hand. The picture disappeared.

'Get me the Kandy Man!' Helen A ordered Daisy K. For the first time she seemed worried.

'You're not unhappy about something,' asked Daisy K smugly.

'I said get me the Kandy Man!' screamed Helen A. Daisy K obediently lifted a receiver from the console, pressed some buttons and waited for the ringing tone of the Kandy Kitchen's telephone before handing the receiver to Helen A.

The Kandy Man hated telephone calls. They invariably led to orders which in turn led to him having to postpone whatever he was doing. So he contemplated the curling, twisty pink and blue telephone for some time before he finally decided to answer it. 'Kandy Man,' he said morosely.

Helen A, annoyed at being kept waiting, dispensed with the niceties of telephone technique. 'I want the Doctor,' she snapped, when she heard the Kandy Man's voice, 'and I want him now. I don't care what you have to do. I don't care how far you have to go.'

The Kandy Man, who had been holding the telephone away from his head to protect his eardrums, spoke into the mouthpiece again. 'That won't be necessary,' he said.

'Why not?'

'Because he's just popped in,' said the Kandy Man, and replaced the receiver. During the conversation he had been watching with interest as the manhole cover in the corner of the kitchen had been slid aside. Then he saw the tip of the Doctor's umbrella come out of the hole, and, attached to the other end, the Doctor himself. Finally he watched the Doctor put the umbrella back into the hole and haul up a human girl.

'Kandy Man,' said the Doctor, doffing his hat, 'I don't believe you've had the pleasure of meeting my friend Ace.' Ace smiled weakly. The Doctor had told her about the Kandy Man, but she still wasn't prepared for the immensely powerful and sinister figure she saw before her. 'She's an expert in calorification, incineration, carbonization and inflammation,' explained the Doctor.

'I beg your pardon,' said the Kandy Man, wiping his hands on his stained lab coat.

121

'She's come to look at your oven.'

Ace scanned the massive bank of ovens occupying the whole length of one wall of the Kandy Kitchen. Only one of them, right at the end, behind the Kandy Man, seemed to be in use. She made a run for it, ducking under the Kandy Man's outstretched arm, and struggled to open the huge furnace door.

The Kandy Man was unperturbed by her actions. 'Has she indeed?' he said, still talking to the Doctor. 'Then she should wait to be asked. Impolite guests get to feel the back of my Kandy hand.' He turned to face Ace, still wrestling with the oven door, and slowly moved towards her, his feet making soft sucking noises with each step he took.

'That may be, Kandy Man,' shouted the Doctor. 'But I've come here to conclude our unfinished business, and I don't like to be kept waiting.' The Kandy Man stopped. The Doctor had interested him. 'Last time you saw me,' continued the Doctor, 'you said you were going to kill me.'

The Kandy Man always found invitations like this hard to resist. 'Really, Doctor?' he said, turning away from Ace and back towards him. 'Thank you for reminding me.'

Ace waited until the Doctor was almost within the Kandy Man's reach. 'I wouldn't give that pimplehead a hundred to one against you, Professor,' she cried, taunting the Kandy Man.

The Kandy Man stopped in his tracks and spoke, quite pleasantly, to the Doctor. 'Pimplehead indeed. I'm disappointed in you, Doctor. I would have expected you to choose your friends more carefully. Still,' he smiled, 'she won't be a friend much longer, will she.' He turned his attentions back to Ace.

'But I think you're a pimplehead too,' said the Doctor.

The Kandy Man was getting irritated. 'I'm finding this all rather tiresome,' he said. He glanced from one to another, and reached into his lab coat pocket for a coin. 'Heads or tails, Doctor?'

'Tails.'

The Kandy Man tossed the coin into the air, caught it

and slapped it on to his wrist. Ace, using the time bought for her by the Doctor, finally managed to prise open the great oven door. The Kandy Man examined the coin, and peeled it off his wrist before it stuck fast.

'Well?' said the Doctor.

But the Kandy Man gave nothing away. 'That would be telling,' he said. And then, showing a surprising turn of speed for a creature of his size he lunged towards Ace. But Ace had been watching him and was ready. She pulled a poker out of the oven and brandished it at the Kandy Man.

'You're playing a dangerous game, Kandy Man,' said the Doctor. 'The tip of that poker is white hot. It would slice through you like a knife through butterscotch.'

The Kandy Man sighed. This was all turning out to be rather more strenuous than he had hoped. 'I have to bow, however reluctantly, to your logic, Doctor,' he said. 'Which leaves me only one choice.' He roared and charged at the Doctor.

'Ace! shouted the Doctor.

She knew what to do. She hurled the poker to the Doctor. It spun through the air, turning over and over, until the Doctor caught it by the cool end.

'Get down, Ace,' he yelled, and slammed down a lever, which supplied gas to the bank of ovens. He thrust the poker into the nearest of them and a great wave of fire sprang from the wall. The Kandy Man yelled as the blast of heat swept him across the kitchen. He crashed to the floor beside the open manhole.

'Time to cool off,' he observed drolly, and slipped down into the pipes.

The Doctor hit the lever again, starving the ovens of gas; the fireball disappeared. 'Ace?' he said, mopping his brow.

'Yes?' she replied, gazing at the manhole.

'How did you know I wouldn't catch the red-hot end?'

'You wouldn't do that, Professor,' she grinned.

The Doctor laughed, and then saw the Kandy Man's coin glinting on the floor where it had fallen. He picked it up, showed it to Ace, wrapped his fingers round it, opened his palm again and it had vanished. Ace was unimpressed; she was more interested in what had happened to the Kandy Man.

The Doctor held out his arm to stop her from peering into the manhole. And then he realized something strange had happened. 'Listen, Ace,' he said.

Ace tried to listen to whatever it was that had caught the Doctor's attention but all she could hear was the sound of her own breathing. 'I can't hear anything.'

'Exactly,' said the Doctor, triumphantly.

'What do you mean?'

'I can't hear anything either,' said the Doctor, leading her upstairs to the street door. 'Come on.'

'What about the Kandy Man?'

The Doctor looked back down at the empty kitchen. 'He'll keep. He's full of colouring, flavouring.' He paused. 'And preservative,' he added, pushing the door open and making his way out into the street.

What the Doctor had heard, or rather hadn't heard, was the sound of muzak, which was so universally present on Terra Alpha, that after a while the only time the inhabitants of the planet noticed it was when it stopped. In the silence following the Kandy Man's abrupt departure from the Kandy Kitchen the Doctor realized that on the previous occasions he had visited the Kandy Kitchen he had always been able to hear muzak filtering down into the kitchen from the speakers in the street outside.

As they came through the door into the street, the reason for the mysterious silence was immediately apparent. Earl and Susan Q were in the street to greet them, standing beneath a loudspeaker dangling from the wall. Susan Q was holding Priscilla P's fun gun. It was obvious that they had been celebrating their victory over Priscilla by using her gun to destroy the muzak machines, symbols of all that they hated about Terra Alpha.

'Blissful, isn't it, Doctor,' said Earl, cheerfully. He nodded at the defunct speaker. 'Silence.'

'Not quite, Earl,' smiled the Doctor. 'I can hear the sound of empires toppling.'

Earl put his arm round Susan Q's shoulders. 'And all thanks to this lady and her fun gun. She can take out a loudspeaker at a hundred paces.'

'Not quite, Earl,' said Susan Q, blushing. But she raised the gun and shot a bullet through the last wire attaching the speaker to the bracket on the wall. The speaker crashed into the street.

Ace watched this with admiration and a certain amount of envy. 'Can I have a go, Professor?'

'Certainly not,' said the Doctor. 'Wanton destruction of public property.' He thought for a moment. 'But in this case, yes,' he said, winking at Ace.

14

The Pipe People had waited in the pipes while Ace and the Doctor confronted the Kandy Man. And they were still waiting when the massive figure of the Kandy Man fell through the open manhole into the pipes. Panicking, they tried to scramble into hiding places. But it was unnecessary. The Kandy Man hurried past them, seeing nothing but the pipe in front of him.

The Pipe People reassembled, brushed themselves down, and unanimously agreed that now the Kandy Man was gone they should take a look around the kitchen. One by one, they followed Wences up through the manhole.

Their attention was caught by a large chart on the wall facing the bank of ovens, which Wulfric quickly identified as a map of the pipes under the city. Traced in pink on the map was the route taken by the fondant surprise on its way to the execution yard. Wences compared this with the direction of the Kandy Man's flight. After some excited exchanges the Pipe People gathered round the wheel used to activate an execution. At a signal given by Wences, they all heaved until the wheel slowly started to move.

Other wheels suddenly began to turn and lights began to flash. A loud rushing noise filled the air. The Pipe People watched the liquid foam as it travelled sluggishly along transparent pipes on its inexorable way towards its victim. The rushing sound increased until it was almost deafening.

'Wicked!' shrieked Wences, unable to contain his excitement.

At that moment Gilbert M came running down the stairs

into the kitchen. He had been making out a report of his version of events in Forum Square when suddenly he had felt in his bones that the Kandy Man was in danger. He saw the Pipe People scampering around the kitchen as they enjoyed the progress of the fondant surprise, and noted the absence of the Kandy Man. It didn't take a genius to work out what had happened.

'Kandy Man,' he said softly. Then he shouted. 'Kandy Man! What have you done to him.' He stared at them, feeling as if a limb had been ripped from his body. Sobbing, he ran up the stairs and out into the open air.

When the Kandy Man had first heard the familiar rumblings in the pipes behind him, he had tried to go faster, to scramble to safety. But then he recalled that he had devised the fondant surprise himself and how ingenious and foolproof he had made it. He stopped and sat down with a certain amount of pride, listening to the rushing sounds getting louder and nearer. 'Ah well,' he said happily, 'I gave it my best shot.' He waited for the end.

The Doctor and Ace had seen Gilbert M rush out of the Kandy Kitchen and head off in the direction of the execution yard, and dashed back into the kitchen to see what had happened. The Pipe People were still celebrating. 'Wulfric,' said the Doctor. 'Wences. What did you do?'

Wulfric pointed rather shamefacedly to the chart on the wall.

'I thought so,' frowned the Doctor, walking over to the chart and examining it. Next to it was a list of ingredients. 'Now let's see,' he said. 'Citric acid, benzoic acid and salicylic acid.' He sighed. 'The Kandy Man won't get very far with that lot following down the pipe.' He considered the Pipe People, wishing they hadn't taken justice into their own hands. 'Come on, Ace,' he said. The Pipe People looked devastated. 'And you, pipe pilots,' said the Doctor, softening.

'Where to now, Professor?' asked Ace.

'Our next port of call.'

Reports of fierce battles around the sugar factories had

127

been flooding into the Happiness Patrol's headquarters, and Helen A, responding to them by deploying the troops which had remained loyal to her, had missed the drama in the Kandy Kitchen. When there was a lull in the fighting, and she told Daisy K to reestablish contact with the Kandy Kitchen, the monitor showed them that it was deserted. Daisy was now at the control console, trying to reach the Kandy Man at other likely locations in the city.

'No reply,' said Daisy K, replacing the receiver.

'He must still be in the Kandy Kitchen,' said Helen A.

'I've already tried there.'

'Then try it again.'

Daisy K punched a button on the console. Once again they saw the familiar picture of the Kandy Kitchen. They watched as the automatic camera roved over the room, seeking out even the darkest corners, and proving that it was quite deserted.

'I wonder where he can be,' said Helen A, trying to make it sound casual. But now that the Happiness Patrol were defecting in their hundreds, she knew that the Kandy Man was her last hope. She took a decision, and headed for the connecting door to her suite. Daisy K got up to follow her.

'Stay where you are, Daisy K,' said Helen. 'I need you in here to keep an eye on things.' She then slipped through the doorway.

Gilbert M had never been down in the pipes, and in truth he was rather scared of them. So when he had worked out what the Pipe People had done to the Kandy Man, he quickly ruled out the possibility of pursuing him under ground. Instead he hurried to the execution yard, hoping that he might be able to patch up the Kandy Man when the fondant surprise finally spewed him out.

But he was too late. When he arrived, the remains of the Kandy Man were already littered across the platform normally reserved for the last moments of Helen A's victims. His robotic metal skeleton was almost intact, lying in a pool of viscous substances, the sugar-based components that had made up the flesh of the Kandy Man, in various stages of decomposition.

Joseph C was bending over the platform when Gilbert stumbled in, exhausted by his run from the Kandy Kitchen. Joseph waved at the mess that used to be the Kandy Man. 'It came down the pipe,' he said helpfully. Gilbert M took one look at the platform and knew that the Kandy Man was finished. He stepped back and looked down, remembering his friend. Joseph C, wrapping round his hand the leash that he was inexplicably carrying – Gilbert looked round the yard but could see no animal – did the same.

After a long period of silence, Joseph turned to Gilbert. Perhaps the fellow would like to talk about it, he thought. 'Close, were you?' he asked Gilbert sympathetically.

Gilbert M summoned up a smile. 'I made him.'

Joseph C was surprised. Only Helen A and Gilbert M had known the true origin of the Kandy Man. 'Really?' said Joseph. 'How very interesting.'

'Only his body,' said Gilbert. 'His mind was very much his own.'

Joseph C knew that this made sense. 'I certainly don't recall the chap ever arriving,' he said.

'He was born in the Kandy Kitchen.'

'Whereas you came from Vasilip,' said Joseph C, 'if memory serves.'

The mention of the name of Gilbert M's home planet brought memories flooding back, memories he hoped had disappeared for ever. Happy memories, of when he had been appointed chief state scientist, the youngest ever to hold the post, and memories of his friendly rivalry with Seivad, the other great scientist on Vasilip. And of how, after years of competition, they had finally worked together, pushing science to new boundaries.

There were unhappy memories, too, of things starting to go wrong. He remembered the king's order that Seivad and he were to be killed on sight; he remembered their flight from the capital, and the lone vigilante who tracked them to their hiding place in the mountains. Gilbert had been out that day, foraging for food. When he returned to their hut he found Seivad wounded and left for dead. Working through the night, Gilbert had managed to save Seivad's mind. The next day he had stowed away on the first flight out of Vasilip which had taken him, and what was left of Seivad, to Terra Alpha. Finally he remembered Helen A's cruel ultimatum, when she had discovered his true identity: create for me a monster out of Seivad, or return to wandering the space lanes looking for a home. Exhausted, Gilbert had complied with her wishes, fashioning the Kandy Man out of the only raw materials at his disposal. And so Seivad had been imprisoned in an executioner's body, his mind twisted with anger and injustice.

Gilbert M turned wearily back to Joseph C. He couldn't face long explanations. 'I was exiled from Vasilip,' he said. I came here with him in a suitcase.'

'Exiled, you say?'

Gilbert M explained briefly. 'I made a mistake. I ran the state laboratories. Without knowing it I developed a deadly new germ. The disease wiped out half the population.'

'Still,' said Joseph pleasantly, 'hardly your fault.' He considered the Kandy Man for a moment. 'Can't you just pack him up and start again?'

Gilbert was tired. 'Not this time,' he said. 'Anyway, he's better off like that. The Kandy Man's gone. There's nothing here for me now.'

Joseph didn't like to see a man so upset. He patted Gilbert's shoulder. 'Chin up, old man,' he said.

Reports of military action at the sugar factories were raining in on Daisy K as she manned the console in the Happiness Patrol's headquarters. She was bombarded with requests from section leaders for reinforcements and strategic decisions. Out of her depth, she yanked off her headphones, leaving the voices to scream their demands into thin air, and ran into the suite to find Helen A packing a suitcase, and humming softly to the muzak floating into the room.

Daisy K was astonished. 'Will you be away long?' she asked.

'Away?' asked Helen A, carefully folding a dress.

'You're packing a suitcase,' said Daisy K. 'I assumed . . .'

Helen A interrupted her. 'Why would I want to go away?'

'I just thought . . . the situation.'

'The situation?' Helen A put the dress down and looked into Daisy K's eyes. 'There's nothing wrong, is there, Daisy K?'

Helen A seemed to have blocked out the events around her but Daisy K knew better than to try to contradict her again. 'No, of course not,' she said. 'Everything's fine.'

The muzak was interrupted by a newscaster. 'Happiness will prevail,' she said. 'Pockets of Happiness Patrol resistance have now crumbled as the drones move through sector eight. One hundred and twelve factories have now fallen to the rebels as they continue their drive westwards.'

But Helen A was not listening. 'As you said, Daisy K,' she said, as the muzak started up again, 'everything is fine. I'm happy,' she said, picking up her suitcase.

'I'm glad you're happy,' said Daisy.

This time, Helen A ordered Daisy to stay in the suite, and passed through into the Happiness Patrol headquarters, closing the door firmly behind her.

Seated at the console, Helen A pressed a series of buttons. The large monitor in front of her lit up. She smiled broadly as she read the message: 'Escape shuttle ready for take-off.'

All the manholes leading from the pipes up into the palace were fitted with heavy padlocks that had tricky combinations. The Pipe People had brought the Doctor and Ace to a manhole leading up to a small room just inside the palace walls, and the Doctor had climbed up the small iron ladder to the underside of the manhole cover.

'Are we under the palace now?' Ace asked him.

'Yes,' said the Doctor, working on the combination.

'This is our way in.' He called to the Pipe People, who were keeping guard with their spears. 'Wences, Wulfric!' They scampered to the foot of the ladder. 'I'm afraid this is where we must say goodbye,' said the Doctor.

'Doctor!' said Wences, clearly disappointed.

'No protests,' said the Doctor. 'Soon you should be able to go back to the sugar fields.'

Wences seemed to be pacified by the prospect of the return to the natural habitat of the Pipe People.

The Doctor stopped fiddling with the lock for a moment, listening to a new sound. The others heard it too. A soft, distant rumbling.

'Something's taking off,' said Ace.

'Yes,' agreed the Doctor. 'Sounds like a shuttle.' He went back to the lock and was soon rewarded with a sweet click as it snapped open.

Helen A stared at the screen in disbelief. The message had changed from 'Escape shuttle ready for take-off' to 'Shuttle in orbit'. There must be a malfunction, she thought, because only she had the means to activate the shuttle.

As she watched the message dissolved into interference, which then gave way to a new message, this time reading, 'Receiving incoming communication.' Helen A gazed at the monitor, transfixed, as Gilbert M appeared, obviously talking from the orbiting shuttle.

'Gilbert M!' snarled Helen A, unwilling to believe that he had hijacked her only means of escape.

'It's all working beautifully, Helen A, as you can see,' said Gilbert M, who had used Vasilip technology to build Helen A the shuttle as part of their bargain, shortly after he had arrived. 'A masterful piece of engineering, even though I say it myself,' he added modestly.

'You betrayed me!'

Gilbert M scratched his chin. 'My only complaint is the company,' he continued, making conversation. 'I don't know how you put up with it,' he said, laughing.

But Helen A still didn't understand. Gilbert M had

created the spacecraft, but she had removed from him the means to fly it. 'How did you get into my escape shuttle?' she demanded.

'That's what I was saying,' Gilbert insisted. 'The captain let me in.'

So it was a conspiracy. 'Who is this captain?' asked Helen A. 'Let me see him.'

The camera panned to the other seat in the shuttle to reveal Joseph C. 'Goodbye, dear,' he said, waving.

Helen A opened her mouth to speak, but no words would come out. She breathed deeply and after a few moments she discovered her voice again. 'What are you doing!' she asked Joseph, too astonished to be angry. Then she remembered where she had left him. 'You're supposed to be waiting for Fifi!'

'Really, dear?' said Joseph, looking down at the leash, which was still wrapped round his hand. 'It must have slipped my mind.' Then the screen went blank as the shuttle shot into the dark void of space, bearing Gilbert and Joseph to new lives on a distant, unknown planet.

Helen was staring in shock at the blank monitor when Daisy K came in. Daisy was puzzled. 'You came back?' she said.

'I never went away,' said Helen, not looking round.

'But I thought I heard . . .' Daisy K, like the Doctor and his party, had heard the unmistakable sound of the shuttle as it was launched.

Helen A switched off the monitor and turned to Daisy, calm and businesslike. 'Really?' she said. 'I didn't hear anything. Is everything still all right?'

Daisy K decided the time had come to end the charade. 'Helen A,' she said boldy. 'You know it isn't. The factories are overrun, the Kandy Man is dead . . .'

'Stop!' shouted Helen A.

'But you must understand. The Doctor is closing on us.'

Helen A covered her ears with her hands. 'Stop!' she shouted. 'I asked you if everything was still all right.'

Daisy looked at her, not replying.

133

'And we're both happy?' asked Helen A.

Daisy K was still silent.

Helen A opened the suitcase and took out a small gun. She levelled it at Daisy. She repeated her question for the last time. 'We are both happy, aren't we?' she said quietly.

Daisy K was saved by a crashing noise from the room above them. Helen A grabbed the suitcase and ran for the door. When she reached it she turned back to Daisy K, who was still standing near the console. 'Happiness will prevail, Daisy K,' she said. She threw the gun across the room to Daisy, and slipped away, heading for the rocket port.

Daisy K caught the gun cleanly, so she was armed and ready to face the Doctor when he slid down the pole into the room from the sleeping quarters of the Happiness Patrol above.

'I was looking for Helen A,' said the Doctor, doffing his hat. 'I don't suppose . . .'

'You're too late, Doctor,' said Daisy K. Her face relaxed into a smile. 'But I'm delighted to see you.' She raised her gun, but a shot rang out before she could fire. Daisy's gun flew from her hand and across the room.

Daisy spun around to see Susan Q at the door covering her with Priscilla's fun gun. Earl was behind her. They had followed the Doctor and Ace into the pipes and the Pipe People had directed them to the open manhole leading into the palace. They had timed their arrival at the nerve centre of the building to perfection.

The Doctor bent down to retrieve Daisy K's gun. 'Who taught you to shoot like that, Susan Q?' he asked.

Susan Q indicated Daisy K with the barrel of the fun gun. 'She did.'

'Thank you, Daisy K,' smiled the Doctor. He tapped on the ceiling with his umbrella. 'All right, Ace,' he shouted, 'you can come down now.'

Ace slid down the pole and ran to the Doctor. 'Are you all right, Professor?'

'Splendid, thank you,' he said.

134

Ace walked over to Daisy K, and looked into her eyes. 'Hello, face-ache,' she said.

Helen A had reached the dark streets on the edge of the city, streets that she would never normally have expected to see – streets where the killjoys had held secret political meetings before the Doctor's arrival. She was tired and afraid as she dragged her battered suitcase behind her, but she was fortified by the tinkling sounds of the muzak emanating from some of the few loudspeakers which had escaped Susan Q's purge. It seemed to Helen A that her empire was still in place while the muzak played.

Even as she drew small crumbs of hope from these thoughts, the muzak stopped. The speakers crackled for a few moments and then the sound of Earl's sad harmonica music sang out, wrapping Helen A in its melancholy. She faltered for a moment, on the point of giving up. But then she took a firm grip on the suitcase and surged on. Whatever she was, she would not go down in history as a quitter.

Helen A guessed accurately that Earl had found the music centre of the palace, which fed music to cities, towns and villages across the entire planet. He was now seated in front of a microphone, pouring his soul out in the music, while Susan Q unravelled the thousands of spools of tape containing the inconsequential sounds that Helen A had inflicted on her people from the first day of her dictatorship. Daisy K had been tied to a chair in the corner of the room. Now she was vainly struggling to escape, almost unable to watch this final, humiliating insult.

The Doctor and Ace had left Susan Q and Earl in the palace while they tracked down Helen A. The Doctor knew where she was headed and quickly worked out her likely route. Unhampered by any baggage, they made good time and soon, hidden in a doorway, they were watching her trudging towards them, pulling the heavy suitcase behind her. They, too, had heard the transition from muzak to

135

blues on the loudspeakers, and knew that Helen A would be at breaking point.

As Helen A walked past the doorway, the Doctor stepped out of the shadows to confront her. 'You can't get away, Helen A,' he said.

Helen A walked on, not even glancing at him. 'There's a scheduled flight in an hour,' she said. 'You can't stop me, Doctor.'

The Doctor stood to one side, allowing her to pass. 'I know I can't. But it's not me you're running away from.'

'Who is it, then?'

'It's yourself. That's why you'll never escape.'

Helen A stopped dead in her tracks and looked at the Doctor for the first time. He sensed that she needed to explain herself. 'They didn't understand me,' she said.

But the Doctor had already seen enough. He needed no further explanations. 'They understood you only too well. That's why they resisted you.'

Helen felt her people had been ungrateful. 'I wanted only the best for them,' she said.

'That's your best, is it?' The Doctor was angry. 'Prisons, death squads, executions.'

'They only came later,' Helen protested. 'I told them to be happy. I gave them a chance. But they wouldn't listen.' She paused, thinking back. 'I know they laughed sometimes, but they still cried, they still wept.'

The Doctor regarded her with pity. 'Don't you ever feel like crying?' he asked softly.

'Of course not, Doctor,' snapped Helen A. She had rid herself of her previous self-doubt and was spouting her philosophy again. 'It's unnecessary. And those who persisted had to be punished.'

'But why?'

'For the good of the majority. For the ones who wanted to take the opportunities that I gave them.'

The Doctor laughed derisively. 'And what were these opportunities that you gave them?' he asked. 'A bag of sweets? A few tawdry party decorations? Bland soulless music?' He stared at her. 'Do these things make you happy?'

Helen A was shaken. It was clear to the Doctor that she hadn't even considered this.

'Of course they don't,' he snapped, answering his own question. 'Because they're cosmetic. Because real happiness is nothing if it doesn't exist side by side with sadness.' He held his hand in the air and the Kandy Man's coin appeared between his fingers. He tossed it into the air. 'See,' he said, showing her the coin. 'Two sides, one coin.'

He held out the coin to Helen, offering it to her, but she knocked his hand away and the coin fell to the ground. She felt the Doctor was patronizing her and was angry again, recovering the old tigerish passion that had destroyed her enemies on her way to power. 'You can keep your coin, Doctor,' she snarled. 'And your sadness. I'll go somewhere else. I'll find somewhere where there is no sadness. A place where people know how to enjoy themselves.'

'I'm sure you will, Helen A,' said the Doctor, 'but it won't be a life worth living.'

Helen A ignored him. 'A place where people are strong – where they hold back the tears. A place where people pull themselves together.'

'Where there's no compassion.'

'Where there's control.'

'You mean a place without love,' said the Doctor.

Helen A looked at the Doctor long and hard. A smile played round the corners of her mouth. 'I always thought love was overrated,' she said. But as soon as she had spoken her expression changed to one of desolation.

'Fifi,' she said simply.

'Fifi?' said the Doctor, puzzled. What had Fifi to do with anything? But now Helen was running past him. He spun round and there indeed was Fifi, dragging herself towards them, with a great gash in her side. He was astonished that she had survived the rock fall but could see that she was barely alive and had undertaken the terrible journey to the surface only so that she could die in the arms of Helen A.

137

'Fifi!' cried Helen A, scooping her up, tears cascading down her cheeks. 'Fifi!' She held her close, rocking her backwards and forwards, like a mother with a baby.

With one last, great effort, Fifi lifted her head to Helen A. But then her strength ebbed, and Helen A, still holding her tight, felt Fifi relax in her arms as she gave up the unequal struggle. Great sobs racked Helen A's body as she buried her head in Fifi's fur, her tears mingling with Fifi's blood.

The Doctor walked back to the doorway where Ace was waiting for him.

'Should we do something, Doctor?' she asked.

'It's done,' he said.

They walked up the street, leaving Helen A to mourn over the body of the only creature she had ever loved.

15

By first light, most of Forum Square had been repainted. Soft colours now mingled with the bright colours preferred by Helen A. Susan Q, Earl and Wulfric had come to say goodbye to the Doctor and Ace. The mood was subdued, but enlivened by the constant bickering of Daisy K and Priscilla P, who were putting the final touches to restoring the TARDIS to its familiar deep blue.

'What's your next stop, Doctor?' asked Earl, when Daisy and Priscilla had finished and disappeared down the street to the execution yard, their next job.

'Good question,' said the Doctor.

But Ace had an idea. 'Can't we go after Joseph C and that toerag Gilbert M?'

'Forget Gilbert M,' said Susan Q. 'It was the Kandy Man who was dangerous.'

'Yes,' agreed the Doctor. 'Hatred, evil, emulsifiers, bigotry, lecithin and non-dairy fats.'

'Stop it, Professor,' moaned Ace. 'You're making me hungry.'

'Right,' said the Doctor, 'it's been a long night. We must be off. How about you, Earl?'

'I'll stay here – to teach this planet the blues again.'

'Thank you for giving them back to us, Doctor,' said Susan Q. The Doctor looked puzzled. 'The blues, I mean.'

He smiled. 'There aren't any other colours without the blues.'

The Doctor doffed his hat to Susan Q and Wulfric and shook hands with Earl, and he watched with Ace as they set off down the street to check on progress in the execution yard, accompanied by the mournful sound of Earl's harmonica.

Ace had discovered a bit of the TARDIS that Daisy and Priscilla had missed and she was rectifying it with a spray can that she had found in her rucksack. 'Are they all right?' she asked.

'Happiness will prevail,' said the Doctor, gently guiding her through the open door of the TARDIS.

Doctor WHO

1963 — 1989

THE COMPLETE ADVENTURES — IN PRINT!

Target Books have published novels based on just about all the Doctor Who stories ever shown on television — plus a few that never quite made it to the screen. Almost 150 books in all — and most of them are still available.

Ask for Target Books at your bookshop — and if you would like an up-to-date list of Doctor Who novels, please send a large stamped addressed envelope to:

The Doctor Who Editor
WH Allen & Co. Plc
175-179 St John Street
London EC1V 4LL

ARE YOU BUYING DOCTOR WHO MAGAZINE?

Every monthly issue of *Doctor Who Magazine* is packed with information about the world's longest running SF television programme, including news, interviews, archives, and a brand new comic strip featuring the current Doctor! Special reports cover subjects such as visual effects, design, merchandise and reviews of all the new Target Books.

Subscribe to thirteen issues of *Doctor Who Magazine* for the price of twelve! Just fill out or copy the coupon below, enclosing a cheque for the appropriate amount (made payable to Marvel Comics Ltd.), to *Doctor Who Magazine* Subscriptions, P.O. Box 500, Leicester LE99 0AA.

Subscription rates as follows: United Kingdom £18.00; Overseas £30.00; US $60.00. Offer expires July 31st 1990; please allow 28 days for your subscription to take effect.